MORE PRAISE FOR
Nothing Looks Familiar

"I've been saying that Shawn's stories shimmer and sparkle
ever since I first encountered them. They are queer in the way all our
interiors are queer—radically singular, cruel, gentle, wrong, vulnerable,
and erotically secret. I don't know another writer like him for facing
down the strange with such warmth of heart."

—Kathryn Kuitenbrouwer, author of *All the Broken Things*

"Here was my experience reading each and every
story in *Nothing Looks Familiar*: I'd arrive—breathlessly and often
shockingly—at its end, and I'd have to set the book down. I'd have
to think through my own assumptions, and how Shawn Syms was
challenging me to look deeper, to find our common humanity, our fear
and fury and joy. His range is incredible; we're in the mind of the kid
who punishes himself for swearing, the heart of the eighty-year-old
woman so desperately wanting to be touched, the hopes that
the meth addict has for her children, and countless others, all drawn in
direct, unflinching, near-cinematic prose. The best story writers ask us to
look past what's familiar. Count Shawn Syms among the best."

—Megan Stielstra, author of
Once I Was Cool and *Everyone Remain Calm*

NOTHING LOOKS FAMILIAR

stories

SHAWN SYMS

ARSENAL PULP PRESS  VANCOUVER

ARSENAL PULP PRESS
Suite 202–211 East Georgia St.
Vancouver, BC V6A 1Z6
Canada
arsenalpulp.com

The publisher gratefully acknowledges the support of the Canada Council for the Arts and the
British Columbia Arts Council for its publishing program, and the Government of Canada (through
the Canada Book Fund) and the Government of British Columbia (through the Book Publishing
Tax Credit Program) for its publishing activities.

Earlier versions of some of these stories have appeared in the following publications: "On the Line"
in *The Journey Prize Stories 21* (McClelland & Stewart) and *PRISM international*; "Family Circus" in
The Winnipeg Review; "Snap" and "The Exchange" in *Little Fiction*; "Get Brenda Foxworthy" in *Boys
of Summer* (Bold Strokes Books); "Taking Creative License" in *Joyland* magazine and *Joyland Retro
Vol. 1 No. 2*; "Man, Woman and Child" in *This Magazine*; and "Three Tuesdays from Now" in *Friend.
Follow. Text. #storiesFromLivingOnline* (Enfield & Wizenty).

This is a work of fiction. Any resemblance of characters to persons either living or deceased is purely
coincidental.

Cover photograph: Getty Images © Shana Novak
Design by Gerilee McBride
Edited by Susan Safyan

Printed and bound in Canada

Library and Archives Canada Cataloguing in Publication:

Syms, Shawn, 1970–, author
    Nothing looks familiar : stories / Shawn Syms.

Short stories.
Issued in print and electronic formats.
ISBN 978-1-55152-570-9 (pbk.).—ISBN 978-1-55152-571-6 (epub)

    I. Title.

PS8637.Y57N68 2014   C813'.6   C2014-904312-0

                                         C2014-904313-9

In memory of Frank Syms (1943–2014)

CONTENTS

ON
THE LINE

I WON'T GO OUT WITH ANOTHER MAN who works on the kill floor. I can't handle the smell of them, or their attitudes. Forget about men from the plant altogether, that's what I should do. It would drastically cut down on my chances for a date though. Maybe a better solution would be to get out of town altogether.

I take a deep breath, inhaling the eucalyptus scent, then immerse my head in hot, soapy bathwater. My knees rise above the water line, the tips of my breasts poke out above water, still covered in suds. Underwater, I rub my temples with both thumbs. I stay submerged as long as I can, until I come up gasping for breath again. Work ended at three-thirty. It's almost ten now, and I'm finally beginning to feel human.

Turning up the tap to add more hot water, I pour silvery conditioner into my hand and lather up my scalp. Run my fingers through the full length of my dark hair, starting at my forehead and tracing behind my shoulders. Touching my scalp, I feel a phantom fingertip—as if the last half inch of my right baby finger were still there.

The accident was over two years ago. Can't complain much; I got $2,700 in insurance money and seven days off work, with pay. I don't even think about it anymore. Except the occasional Friday night—like tonight—when I drag myself to the Ox for cheap beers. Even then, I only think about it for a second, reminding myself it's one less nail to paint. A lot worse coulda happened.

In the grit of a dive or between sweaty sheets, most guys don't notice. Some men I've dated took weeks to mention the finger. Then again, roughnecks aren't much for holding hands or paying close attention to you. Some don't even kiss.

I ease my head back under to rinse out my hair. I'll be in this town till Dad dies. Don't know how long that'll be. He's taken to falling though. He needs me; living right downstairs has come in handy more than once. Valerie got to escape to Vancouver once she got married. I'll get there too someday.

What'll I even do in BC? I've been cutting meat so long I don't know what else I'm fit for. Maybe lick my wounds and go on pogey for a while? That's hard to imagine. I've always had a job. Val stays at home raising three boys, and I don't envy her. I like to work.

You get used to the plant. You cope. I wield a sharp knife all day long. It's ridiculous, I know, but sometimes I pretend I'm slitting fabric to make little girls' dresses instead of carving carcasses into steaks. Agnes, who works next to me, sings Sudanese songs to help get through the day. She taught me one, called "Shen-Shen." I asked her once what that song is about. "Life is unfair, Wanda. That is what it is about," she said, and went back to singing. Agnes sends money to her mother and father in Juba every month via Western Union. Can't complain about the wage. Fifteen dollars an hour is nothing to sneeze at. The men you meet though. Christ.

Last guy I dated from Slaughter was Karl Willson—a blond behemoth, Prairie farming stock. He was twenty-four, six-three, and very strong—so he was quickly recruited for the harshest job on the kill floor. He's a stunner and sticker: he kills live cattle and drains their blood. I don't think less of guys in Slaughter because their jobs are dirtier than mine. The rest of us can't feel holier-than-thou about chopping steaks, filling sausage links, or grinding burger meat. The reason I don't like Karl is he's a prick.

He came to Alberta a few months ago from Saskatchewan with his younger brother, who got hired to dress carcasses. Karl was well-suited to a job as a cutthroat. He didn't mind killing; he liked it. He was fast. Speedy workers are the company's wet dream.

We only dated for a few weeks. Karl was brooding and edgy. That made for rough, satisfying sex—but I knew something bad would spring from his constant, simmering anger. One night at the drive-in, I teased him about something—I think it was a cowlick that made his hair look funny—and he punched me hard in the face. I don't put up with bullshit—that was the end. We haven't spoken since.

He got moved to B shift. That means I work days and he works nights. When I go to the Ox on a Friday, he's usually not there because he can only make last call by coming right from the plant. He sometimes does, the need to drink outweighing the duty to clean himself up first. The smell of Processing isn't as bad as Slaughter, but I never go to the bar without taking a long bath first.

Standing up to dry myself, I close my eyes a sec. Hope I don't run into Karl tonight. I shouldn't be going out—it's the height of summer, so we're on a six-day week at the plant. I need to be there tomorrow morning at seven, even though it's a Saturday. But I need something to make me forget for a while.

Pulling a towel off the rack, I dry my breasts, belly, the insides of my legs, and bottoms of my feet, and then scrub at my wet hair with the efforts of nine determined fingertips.

The harsh blare of the alarm clock seeps into my consciousness through the hot haze of slumber. I stretch across Makok's broad, dark shoulders to finger the snooze button. Unable to stifle a belch that reeks like last night's whiskey sours, I slump back for nine more minutes of rest, draping my arm across the width of his back. He stops snoring, but doesn't stir.

Morning's light streams through the bedroom window, and I squint. Makok works on Karl's floor, but I don't think they're friends. His wife does dayshift on the line. She's not in my section, but I can see her from where I stand at the boning table. I've seen the two of them at the IGA together; they've both worked at the plant for a few months now.

I think back to last night, and don't recall much. Makok smiling at me as he leaned over the pool table, cue in hand. Asking him to buy me a drink, though I can afford my own liquor. Flattering compliments in halting English. More drinks. His brown eyes locked with my own, an unspoken decision to go ahead.

He faces away, hugging a pillow. I scan his smooth back, visually tracing its one blemish, a three-inch curved white scar across his right shoulder. Must have been a meat hook; that's common. Or something that happened back home—like many at the plant, he's from Sudan. I'm not going to ask.

The alarm buzzes again. Makok shakes awake; both of our hands reach for the noisemaker this time. He smacks the top of the clock and then grabs my fingers.

He turns, and our eyes meet. I lean toward him; we kiss. He pulls his bulky frame onto mine, and I welcome the pressure. We fuck one more time, fiercely and quickly. Before the alarm sounds again, we're done. Makok eases out of me, strokes my cheek, then abruptly pulls himself to his feet and stands naked above me, a drizzle of semen still hanging off the tip of his foreskin.

"Mende is pregnant." He walks to the bathroom.

I sit on the toilet and piss while Makok showers; I put out a clean towel. He doesn't offer me a ride to work—he leaves while I'm in the shower. I tie my hair into a loose braid and throw a sweater into my knapsack. Hot as it is outside, my part of the plant is refrigerated.

I pop four ibuprofens on my way out the door, hop into my Civic, and head for the plant. I crack the window. It's too hot not to, but you don't open it very far. The closer you get to the plant, the more the air smells like shit. Bosses call it "the smell of money." No matter which way the wind blows, you can't escape it.

The locker room smells like wet sawdust, and it's crowded. The air's humid with steam emanating from the shower stalls at the end of the room. On a bench between two rows of lockers, I'm surrounded by women. I recognize some but have never talked to them. You can't know everybody in a plant of 2,000 people. Once we're suited up, it's hard to recognize anyone.

Lockers are assigned in numerical order based on hire date and then reassigned because of turnover—not everyone can handle this job. All around me, women chatter, yell, laugh—none of it in English. You get used to that.

I put on my gear in the same order every morning. First, the yellow rubber boots. Next, I pull on my steel mesh apron. It runs from my shoulders to my knees. I reach around to tie it in the back, drawing my head to my chest. There, I catch my first whiff. Though I scrubbed it at the end of yesterday's shift, my apron still hosts the faint but dizzying scent of bull's blood.

I hear a rumble from the shop floor; they're turning on the grinders and getting ready for the shift to start. I check my pockets for earplugs. I put on rubber sleeves that run from my wrists to my elbows, a hairnet, then my bump cap—a yellow construction helmet. Plastic safety goggles hang from my neck by a nylon cord; I'll put them on once I'm on the line. I grab my long, thin knife and stuff it into the waist pocket of the apron. Thank God I sharpened it yesterday. With this hangover, I'd cut myself if I tried to today.

Last, thick rubber gloves, with a crumpled paper ball jammed into one fingertip to keep it from flopping or getting caught in anything. All around me, women who've arrived late crowd in and clamber into the same uniform. We have to be on the line when it starts up.

Wading through the crowd and the roaring machines, I arrive at the boning table to find my co-workers already in position. With a smirk, Kwadwo calls out in his West African–accented baritone.

"Wanda, you look like you were up late," he says in a chastising tone.

My shoulders slump. Then I puff out my chest. "I was with your dad last night, Kwadwo. I hope you have as much energy in bed as him!"

Kwadwo giggles like a tickled schoolboy. "My father is fifty-six—and he still lives in Ghana. No wonder you are tired..."

"I went out to the Ox for a few—but not much was going on," I confess.

"As long as you weren't with Kwadwo's father—or any other fathers—then it is good," Agnes pipes in, arching an eyebrow as she adjusts her hairnet over a short-cropped Afro.

Agnes is a generation older than me, but the Sudanese community is close-knit. Could she be friends with Makok and his pregnant wife?

She smiles and gives me a friendly elbow. "Use protection, or you will *make* someone a father!" I grin, relieved.

Next to me, Kwadwo, Agnes, and three girls from Newfoundland work at our compact boning table. We're short one man, a French Canadian, the nephew of Mr Leger, the floor supervisor. Funny that our table is mostly whites—we're a minority on the floor. That's another thing you get used to.

With another clickety-clack rumble, the line kicks into gear. Meat moves into the room from the kill floor downstairs. Along the west wall, enormous whole cattle emerge from the trapdoor, suspended from above by hooks that pierce one of their back limbs. The men at the front of the room take them down one by one and begin to cut.

First, off with their heads. Then, out with their guts. Next, off with their hides. The carcasses hit three other cutting tables before reaching ours. We get manageable, medium-sized slabs ready to be reduced to supermarket-grade cuts. The first will reach our table in just under ten minutes. Several hours of slicing and dicing later, we get lunch at eleven o'clock. I'm so used to separating meat from bones I could do it in my sleep.

Mid-morning, I glance at the bone-shiners' table further down the line. There, a group of women wield electric knives to remove excess meat from bones before they're sent to Rendering. It's hard to tell anyone apart, between the mouth protectors, goggles, hairnets, and helmets, but I think I recognize Makok's wife Mende among the dozen African women at the table. Most chat and smile while they work—with one tall, rigid exception.

At lunch I sit with Agnes, Kwadwo, and Kathy, one of the girls from our group. The cafeteria fare is bearable today: lasagna and fruit salad. We keep things light—no sex, religion, or politics at the lunch table. My aching, dehydrated brain is glad for that. Normally, I love listening to Agnes talk—she's passionate about her homeland—but I couldn't cope right now.

Taking my tray to the garbage bin, I feel an object thunk onto my back. Turning around, I look at the floor and see a grape from someone's fruit salad. A loud guffaw, and then a big, blond dickwad is in my face—Karl's brother, Kevin Willson. He has a v-shaped scar on his cheek and the smile of a carved pumpkin with one front tooth missing.

"Oh, sorry, Wanda. I was aiming for the trash. Guess I missed."

I offer a fake smile.

"Hey, heard you had a busy night. Up late, weren't you?" He sneers. "But you like the dark, don't you?"

That fucking piece of shit. I didn't see him at the bar last night. I shove him out of my way and head back to the floor.

Leger approaches our table as we get ready to go back to work, a young woman in tow. She looks about nineteen, Vietnamese probably, with a very pretty face. She won't last long—she'd be better off in another section. This girl is too short. She'll have to reach upward to make all her cuts. The boning table is designed for people of average height; she'll end up with very sore shoulders.

"Kids, this is Anh. Show her the ropes." With that, he walks away. From behind, it looks like he's picking his nose.

Agnes and I exchange a knowing look. But she smiles when she turns to Anh.

"Where are you from, girl?"

Her voice is a whisper but I manage to hear because she's right next to me. "Cambodia."

"Pull your face mask over your mouth, Anh. I'll show you what to do."

Anh exhales visibly. Agnes has a way of making people comfortable. We all pull our face masks on and get to work. Because of staggered lunch breaks, meat has begun to pile up.

I pick up the first piece and carve, glancing from time to time to watch Agnes and Anh. The girl's cuts are tentative, which is to be expected at the start. Given the jostling from the other tables when things get busy, she'll likely cut herself today. Might as well get her first self-slice out of the way. In contrast to boisterous Agnes, singing and carving next to her, Anh looks fragile. I fear one slit from a sharp knife might cause her to completely disassemble.

Just as Anh gets the hang of things, a loud scream erupts from a table ten feet away. A tall white guy grasps at the red gush of blood coming out of his right biceps. His still-buzzing hock cutter, a hand-held version of a small buzz saw used to slice the limbs off cattle, bounces onto the table in front of him. The electric saw falls onto the concrete floor, glancing off the woman next to him. Shit. Continuing to cut my meat, I watch Leger rush over with a nurse, face riddled with anxiety. I know the bastard's worried about keeping up the speed of the line, not some poor sucker's hacked limb. It wasn't fully severed, anyway. I put my slices into a grey plastic tub, put it on the belt, and grab my next piece of meat.

Anh has dropped her knife to the ground. She watches with widened eyes as the tall man, now hunched over with a white towel pressed against his red and sopping shirt sleeve, is led away by the nurse, sobbing. Meat continues to pile up on the belt in front of us.

Agnes reaches down to grab Anh's knife off the wet floor and holds it lightly by the blade, pointing its handle back at the young woman. She gestures to Anh with the handle. "Anh, you can't stop."

Anh continues to stare mutely toward the hock area, where everyone else is busily back at work with a tiny bit more room per person. Agnes puts the knife into Anh's gloved hand, closes her hand around it, and gently turns her back to face the boning table.

"You *can't* stop." Agnes sighs and looks in my direction, then picks a piece of meat up off the belt and places it in front of Anh, who looks down at it and starts to cut.

The guy is back on the line two hours later. I go into autopilot for the rest of the day. I'm no longer slicing meat; I'm assembling a simple, elegant wedding dress out of *peau de soie*, an A-line with pleats that run from the waist to the feet. No frilly train, but it has a subtle band of patterned lace around the waistline. Sleeveless, but not low-cut, with thin straps. Pretty but unassuming. And the sheerest, most delicate bridal gloves. No fancy patterns, basic white, and they cut off just before the elbow.

The day ends. I hope Anh comes back tomorrow. We need the extra hands at the boning table. I head for the locker room. Pushing my way numbly through the all-female mass, I reach my locker and pause. My combination lock's been snipped with a bolt cutter. I remove it and pull open the door.

The severed head of a dead calf lolls lazily on the top shelf of my locker. Most of its hair has been shaved off, but tufts still cling to its floppy, oversized ears. Both lips have been removed, exposing its skeletal teeth. Its fat, amputated tongue has been stuffed back into its mouth, and it sticks out at an abnormal angle. It smells like vomit. The flesh around the base of the head is mottled and bloody. Along the hacked neckline, two flies sit and feast.

Fucking gross. I slam the locker door shut with all my strength. It bounces back open, impelling the raunchy odour back in my face. With the force of the jolt, the calf's head bounces and tips forward. It topples out of the locker and heaves onto my yellow rubber boot. With a fearful bolt of adrenaline, I kick it down the row of lockers. It comes to a stop at the other end of the hall, where a group of women are coming out of the showers. They stop en masse, emitting yelps and grunts of disgust, looking over at me, and swearing. The calf's tongue fell out of the head when I kicked it; it lies on the ground a few feet away. I crumple to the bench and find myself crying for the first time in years. I wish I were anywhere but here.

I step out of the women's locker room an eternity later. As I head for the exit, a deep voice calls out to me.

"Hey, slut." Karl Willson stomps my way with a crooked sneer on his lips.

I cross my arms in front of my chest. "What the fuck do you want?"

He answers in sing-song. "Is Princess having a bad day?" Karl reaches forward suddenly and shoves my crossed arms so hard I fall backward to the floor. He leans in, and I cover my face quickly. He's yelling in my ear. "What? That black bitch show you what a fucking cow you are?"

I kick him in the shin, a glancing blow, and he steps back. I scramble to my feet. A dozen passersby have slowed or stopped. "What the fuck, Karl!"

"Kevin told me what you did last night, you fucking whore."

The crowd begins to filter away. Another lover's spat. Happens all the time.

"Those people believe in revenge. You better watch out."

"Karl, you're full of shit..."

He spits in my face and walks away. Two women approach, not speaking English. I climb to my feet, recognizing Agnes's voice.

She wears a white blouse, acid-wash jeans, and a faded denim jacket. Next to her stands a tall woman with a pretty face marred by dark circles under her eyes. A dark-green, patterned scarf covers her hair and drapes across her shoulders. She wears a simple white dress. I notice the slight curve of her belly. Makok's wife.

"Wanda, this is my friend, Mende."

I glance downward, then look up at her, my face flushed.

"How are you, Mende?" I manage.

"It is nice to meet you." Her heavily accented English is stilted and formal.

Agnes turns to me. "We're going to church. There are things we need to speak to the pastor about. Maybe you'd like to come with us."

"I'm sorry, Agnes. I need to go make dinner for my father." I look at my feet and back at the two of them. Mende appraises me.

"I heard what happened, Wanda. I thought some spiritual guidance might be a help."

I pause. "You know what happened?"

"At your locker."

I exhale. "A stupid prank. Some joker from the kill floor."

"I believe things happen for a reason, Wanda. If you don't want to come now, you could attend our Sunday-morning service." She touches Mende's arm before adding, "It can help when troubling things happen."

I decide something. "Agnes, I'd join you, but I'll be packing. Dad and I are moving to Vancouver. We leave Monday."

Agnes breaks into a sudden grin. "I can't believe you didn't tell me!"

"No one knows."

"It's time you saw the world." Agnes came from Africa and had lived in Newfoundland for years before coming here. "What are you going to do in the big city—work in a butcher shop?"

"I'm going to be an apprentice to a dressmaker." I realize this by saying it aloud for the first time.

Mende appears distracted, but offers Agnes a confused look. Agnes speaks to her quickly, pointing to me several times. I realize she's translating the conversation we just had. Karl lied—I doubt he could have said anything to Mende. He must've snuck in when the locker room was empty and busted into my locker himself. Whatever.

I embrace Agnes. Mende turns to me and says, "Good luck." The two of them walk away. Men and women stream past in the opposite direction by the dozens, on their way into the plant for B shift.

Better get home and tell Dad, I think. I leave the building and walk alongside the chain-link fence that leads from the plant to the parking lot. I can't remember where I parked my Civic. I scan the sea of parked cars, and nothing looks familiar.

FOUR
PILLS

"I'M GONNA HAVE A GOOD TIME TONIGHT," Adam announced
to the empty park. *Even if I only have five bucks to my name.*
Once Shaggy shows up, we'll get everything sorted.

Adam perched on the swing in a desolated children's play
set behind the towering, unlit greenhouse at Allan Gardens.
His broad frame fit snugly between the two sets of chains. He
stroked his stubbly chin and wiped the sweat off his forehead.
A dirt-speckled Canada Coach bus sped past, leaving purple
exhaust to hang in the humid air.

The play set was a rusty shambles. Adam had never seen
kids in this park. Even during the day, few parents would
consider it a safe space. Instead, it was a nighttime playground for crack heads, whores, and homos. *And me too*,
Adam appended, kicking at the moist near-muck at his feet,

unleashing its sticky earthen odour. *Where the fuck is Shaggy?* he asked himself.

He'd started hanging out in the park a couple months ago, after losing his last warehouse job. The welfare cheque stretched to meet his costs, but barely. After rent, he was left with $123 to get through the month. It was a week till cheque day, but Adam wasn't worried. He could rustle up extra cash. He wasn't even thinking about the rest of the week. Just tonight. It was Sunday night, the ragged edge of the weekend, and Adam had no reason to get up early the next day.

He'd never been good at keeping friends and didn't know why Shaggy liked him. They'd met in Allan Gardens. Adam had been moping on a bench along one of the tree-lined paths that ran through the park. It was better than sitting alone in his basement apartment in the rooming house down the street.

The night they met was the first time Adam tried to buy some rock in the park. Scared shitless, he approached a guy he'd seen dealing crack along the park's pathways. The man laughed in Adam's face but still did the deal. "Did you assume I would have it because I'm black?" he asked, voice dripping with sarcasm. Before Adam could get home with his twenty-dollar piece, he was jumped by two skinny white dudes with shaved heads and scarred faces. Shaggy showed up and got them to lay off. The two brothers, Adam later learned, ran a scam with the first guy to rip off anyone they knew was green.

A lot of people had made Shaggy's acquaintance. He was usually holding drugs of one sort or another; he wasn't a full-on dealer, but he sold on the side. He knew all the hookers on the stroll and most of the crackheads in the park. Once they walked past Filmores strip club together, and Adam was sure he saw a cop sitting in a cruiser nod at Shaggy as they passed.

Shaggy was mysterious; Adam didn't even know where he lived. Shaggy could be a rich kid from Forest Hill slumming in the park. When they hung out, anything felt possible—if only for that moment. Adam decided from the outset not to ask any questions. As long as Shaggy brought the party, he would be there. He didn't mind being a follower.

A nearby echoing boom was followed by a slow creaking sound. Adam looked up and saw a man with slender eyebrows and an even thinner moustache prop open the enormous wooden door of the nearby church. The man looked in his direction and frowned. Adam spat on the ground. The minister turned around, disappearing into the hole left by the arched doorframe. The church, fashioned of worn, blackened stones, had a medieval air. A single lean spire thrust upward like a wagging finger.

Beyond Jarvis Street Baptist, Adam saw a woman in a skimpy, shocking-pink outfit emerge from Hooker Harvey's and begin a jittery stroll north. The first working girl of the evening was out. She looked pretty compared to the crack whore from Adam's building. Once he found that skank screwing a burly, greasy guy in the back alley up against his own apartment door—at ten in the morning. At least the girl outside Harvey's was wearing makeup.

Adam glanced left and saw a shrunken old woman with tobacco-stained hair make her stooped way along the asphalt path surrounding the playground. She had a wooden cane in one hand, an oversized canvas bag in the other. He could already detect her BO. He knew her by sight; maybe in her fifties but ground down by life, the woman was a decrepit fixture around here.

A muffler-less Volkswagen sputtered down Gerrard. Then the park was quiet again, except for the rasp of a breeze through its thick oaks, filling the air with hoarse whispers. All that would change in an hour, as the sun sank and the moon rose.

Traffic would grow dense and slow. Windows rolled down, the air would fill with music from Euro-disco to Led Zeppelin blaring from car stereos. People would be looking for action, summer stir-crazy. The dealers would be out. Loose handfuls of people would languidly migrate through the park. Those from Adam's shit neighbourhood would cross from south to north, looking for greener pastures. Those slumming for the weekend would pass them heading from north to south, looking for a chunk of crack or bag of smack to take back to their chichi Bay Street apartments. Those people were likely to take the same journey to Queen and Sherbourne more than once before the sun came up.

The lopsided shrew had stopped on the other side of the wrought-iron fence separating the playground from the rest of the park. She stared at him. The old bitch opened her mouth, and a child's singsong came out—a child on barbiturates. "Can you spare any change?" She dragged each word out, making it last over several seconds. Adam ignored her. She sounded like a clown but looked like Methuselah in a stinky green sweater.

"Can you spare a cigarette?" Adam grimaced, looking away.

"Cocksucker." She spat from a toothless mouth and limped back in the other direction.

Behind her, a short, stocky man with a precise military haircut trudged through the park. He knew the guy, who wore a bus-driver's TTC uniform. The man nodded and smiled at Adam. He nodded back but quickly looked away.

Smack in the middle of it all was the bulky greenhouse, mostly ignored by the park's night-time inhabitants. Dense, leafy trees lined its western wall. That made it popular with fags, who began to stream toward the park from a nearby gay bar around midnight on the weekends. Some diehards showed up every night, marching a hypnotized circle around the length of the greenhouse with two lingering stops: the tree cover along the west wall and a nearby darkened alcove.

Adam had let a faggot or two suck his cock here, on nights when he couldn't sleep and needed to get off. *These guys are a public convenience*, he told himself, *like a urinal to piss in*. Just a place to put his load. He'd braced himself against a gnarled tree trunk and kept his eyes closed the few times it had happened. He'd been high, and it was a way to get rid of something his body wanted out. That's all. He could never imagine telling Shaggy.

A bell chimed from the nearby steeple. Adam watched a trickle of grey-haired men in decomposing suits escort elderly women in faded dresses and oversized hats into the church for the seven p.m. service. The wrought-iron gate behind him squeaked.

"Hey, dude, sucked off any horse dongs here lately?" With an impish giggle, Shaggy ran toward Adam and tried to push him off the swing. Adam leapt to his feet. Still laughing, Shaggy pushed the swing to one side and tried to tackle him. Longhaired Shaggy was tall but lean and not very strong; Adam lifted him off the ground from behind and easily tossed him into the dirt. Then he squatted down and farted in his face. He smiled, happy he wasn't alone anymore.

"Aw, that reeks. Fuck you!" Shaggy grasped at a pile of dirt and tossed it at Adam's face before hauling himself to his feet. Shaggy waved his hands in the air to clear away Adam's fart, but he was still grinning.

"Let's go for a walk," he said.

Adam followed. They left the playground and walked away from the busy churchyard to the deserted eastern end of the park. It looked deserted at first glance, but as they walked the asphalt path, tiny movements became visible. By a far-off tree, a woman lay on top of a man and kissed him passionately. Both looked fully clothed. From another path, they heard laughter. Three men sat on a bench passing a bottle of Jack Daniel's. Behind them, a fourth faced away and pissed in the grass, steadying himself with effort.

"I need to take my mind off things tonight. Feel like having some fun?"

"Yeah." Adam paused. "What's wrong, though?"

Shaggy ran one hand through his bangs before answering. "My brother."

When he and Shaggy partied, they talked more about their childhoods than the present. Shaggy had mentioned his older brother a couple times lately. Bladder cancer.

Four Pills

"Oh." Adam nodded, but didn't say more. He'd learned to leave it up to Shaggy to decide when he wanted to talk about something.

"I've got some fun lined up for tonight," Shaggy said, all smiles again.

"Rock?" Adam got excited. It was weeks since he'd smoked any crack. He loved the intense, uplifting high. He tried to control the electrified butterflies flitting in his stomach.

"Maybe. Depends if we can line up some cash. In the meantime…" He reached into his pocket and put his hand into the glow of a streetlight.

In his palm were four tablets, marked with the word "Roche" and a number two surrounded by a circle. The moon above them was barely a sliver, and each pill reminded Adam of a star. They were a constellation in Shaggy's hand.

Four roofies. Hyped on the TV news as a "date rape" drug, they were strong downers. Shaggy sometimes sold them for five bucks apiece to guys in the park or spun-out dudes wandering around the John Innes Centre. They brought on sleep after too much crack. Adam guessed the presence of Shaggy's "little helpers" might indeed mean there would be some rock to be smoked tonight. Adam's pocket held his asthma-inhaler crack pipe, which he'd brought out with him, just in case.

He smiled. "Think we might need those pills later on?"

"Or…" Shaggy paused. "We could save them for someone else. If we met some chicks…"

Adam let the words sink in. He wasn't keen on challenging Shaggy, but didn't know how to respond. "Really?"

31

"Hey, bro, it's not so bad." Shaggy replied. "I've only done it with ladies who were into me anyway. For some girls, it's the only way they can come; they're too self-conscious. I can tell by the smile I leave on their faces." A stoner kid in a green lumber jacket rode past them on a motocross, scattering pebbles as his tires skidded by.

"Or," Shaggy said, "we might need them ourselves later. That depends on money. I don't have anything. We'd need to go see Jamie." The guy Adam had bought crack from the first time. Adam bristled at the mention of his name. Shaggy noticed and laughed loudly, then stopped.

"Here's a chance for some cash," he said in a quieter tone.

Up ahead on another path that merged into their own, a man walked briskly, alone. Adam recognized his squat frame; that fag bus driver from earlier. He'd changed from his blue-and-grey uniform into a typical gay-bar outfit: a red-and-black plaid shirt, too-tight Levis, and maroon cowboy boots. The pants and shirt looked neatly pressed. You didn't need to guess twice what kind of place he was headed to. Maybe it was country-and-western night.

Shaggy dropped his voice to a whisper. "I'll distract him, you get him." He sprinted forward until he'd passed the guy by a dozen feet, then stopped and turned to face him.

Adam froze. Shaggy wanted to roll the fag. He just wished it wasn't that particular guy. This could get embarrassing. Shaggy approached the man. At least a decade their senior, he looked in his mid-thirties. "Hey, sir, excuse me. Do you know what time it is?"

Totally lame—but all he was doing was stalling him so Adam could sneak up without being noticed. They'd done this before. Adam watched from behind. The man's reply sounded wary.

"No…I don't have a watch on."

"Are you serious, man? I'm late to meet my girlfriend. What time was it when you left home? I think I'm in big shit. Come on."

He faced the fag the whole time, walking backward as the guy inched forward, Shaggy doing a subtle dance in front of him, slowing him down. His words were really intended for Adam, to urge him forward.

Adam glanced around. A few feet away he saw a discarded ginger-ale bottle. He grabbed it and ran toward the man from behind, raising his arm in the air. The guy turned just as Adam was about to strike him. "Hey, what's going on, Ad—?"

Before he could finish, Adam brought the bottle down on the man's skull as hard as he could.

He didn't fall to the ground or cry out. At best he seemed dazed. Adam took another look at the large bottle in his hand. It was made of plastic, not glass. *Christ, I'm stupid*, he thought. For a surreal second, no one moved. Then the guy bolted past Shaggy and ran toward the park's edge. The guys took off after him, but the fat little queer had a head start—and their hearts weren't in it anyway. After ten seconds or so, they both trailed off. Adam leaned against a huge oak and caught his breath.

Shaggy gave him a curious look, and didn't say anything. Then he picked up an imaginary plastic pop bottle in his right hand, raised it over Adam's head, and brought it back down. And yelled "Bonk!" He burst out laughing. Adam blushed. Soon he was laughing too. "At this rate," Shaggy said, "we won't be partying till *next* weekend."

Shaggy stopped and peered across the street. "Hey, lookit," he said. She wore a pink latex top that was little more than brassiere and slinky black short shorts. It was the hooker Adam had seen earlier. Shaggy donned an on-the-make smile, said, "Follow me," and zipped across the street. Adam followed him.

Shaggy sauntered over to where the hooker stood as Adam tried to catch up.

"How you doing, Shauna?" he said, all feigned nonchalance.

Shauna was a very tall woman. She was bigger than Shaggy, though at least four of her inches came from black stiletto pumps. Her lids were painted in pale blue eye shadow, her lips in a bubble-gum pink that matched her bustier. She spat out a piece of gum. Shauna looked down her nose at Shaggy and said, in what Adam thought was a Caribbean accent of some sort, "Bitch, you can't afford me."

Her pupils narrowed, then opened wide. She threw her arms around Shaggy and picked him up off the ground. Adam watched in amazement as Shaggy's face was crushed against her breasts. As Shaggy reciprocated her embrace and let his hands quickly roam around her back, she put him down and said in a warning tone, "Hey, just don't touch the hair," tossing her long, chemically straightened locks behind her shoulders and flashing a toothy grin. She glanced over at Adam and winked. He couldn't take his eyes off her, but remained a few safe feet away.

Shaggy quietly engaged Shauna in small talk so that Adam couldn't make out what they were saying. Shaggy touched her arm and then stepped back to join Adam, giving Shauna an overblown, lurid once-over to which she responded with a haughty, heavy-lidded glare.

"See you later, sweet thing," Shaggy called out, gesturing to Adam to return to the park.

"Yeah. Show me the money, bitch!" Shauna called out in a mocking tone.

Adam dodged several lanes of traffic on Jarvis to catch up. "Shag, is she a transsexual or something?" Across the street, the bold Amazon ignored them now, her eyes focused on oncoming cars. A dark-blue Mercedes slowed in front of her.

"Bro, that's a pretty personal question. You'd need to pay to even *ask* her." Shaggy replied. "She's spun out of her mind on speed right now. You didn't notice her track marks? If she *were* packing a tool, there's no way she'd be able to get it up now," he offered, adding in a mischievous tone, "She used to be my babysitter when I was a kid. Makes a lot better money now from what she told me."

Shaggy was undoubtedly shitting him about the babysitter bit, but Adam didn't bother to call him on it. As they approached the playground, Adam's eyes honed in on the only other person nearby. That old hag. She was sitting on the swing.

Adam had always hated that bitch. He saw his chance to recover from making a fool of himself in front of Shaggy before. He tapped Shaggy on the shoulder and brought a finger to his lips. As Shaggy watched, he entered the open gate into the playground and tiptoed closer.

Her brown wooden cane and canvas bag leaned on the swing set beside her. Adam paused right behind her, then lurched forward, made a grab for her bag, and ran like hell.

"Hey!" The astounded woman bellowed as he sprinted away. "Faggot! Faggot! *Faggot!*" she screamed. She jumped up, grabbed her cane, and lobbed it at Adam, striking him hard in the calf. Pain sliced through his leg and Adam let out an agonized yell but kept going, breaking into a staggering but determined limp. The bitch stood there and shrieked.

Shaggy detoured around the playground and ran to meet Adam at the other end of the park. They stopped at a bench right at the entrance. A police car drove past with sirens blaring. Ignoring it, they plopped the hefty bag onto the bench and began to rummage.

A can of Lemon Pledge. A bunch of old newspapers. What looked like a half a meatball sub neatly wrapped in wax paper. A handful of packets of K-Y Jelly. A balled-up wad of bloody gauze. And a small change purse covered in large, gaudy rhinestones.

Adam pulled it out, snapped it open, and saw a clutch of twenties inside. He *knew* that bitch wasn't really poor. He turned to Shaggy and smiled. Shag patted him on the back. Adam felt vindicated. He put the change purse in his pocket, and tossed the canvas bag back into the park for the old woman.

The night now felt wide open. Adam trembled with adrenaline.

He felt he'd done something right for the first time in years. Then he looked down and saw that his leg was oozing blood right down into his shoe.

It wasn't gushing out, and he only lived two blocks away. He turned to Shaggy and smiled. "I gotta get cleaned up. Let's go back to my place."

On the way, Shaggy ran into the beer store, and Adam leaned against the building and waited. He watched Shaggy through the window as he paid for six tall cans of Crest Super. The pimple-faced clerk put them into a black plastic bag. Ten-percent alcohol, Crest was a great way to start a party. Adam got tanked pretty easily anyway; he was a certified lightweight. Some coke would balance things out. On the way home, Shaggy said now that they had some money, he should bring Shauna to Adam's.

"Let's wait and see just how much money we've got," Adam proposed as they turned off Sherbourne into the back alley behind his basement apartment. He knew Shaggy wanted to use the money—or was it those pills?—on his hooker friend.

"I've been with Shauna before, and she'll blow your fucking mind, bro."

They reached the back of the low-rise. A concrete stairwell led down a few feet to the entrance to Adam's unit. Adam unlatched the gate, and they walked down the stairs. They entered the tiny apartment. Adam groped for the switch.

They stepped into the dimly lit underground space with its brown carpet and low ceiling. The apartment was two adjoined rooms, the kitchen and the bedroom, which had a tiny bathroom off it. The windows were all at the top of the walls, only an inch from the ceiling. The view showed the first six inches of the laneway.

A pile of dishes sat in the sink, remnants of last night's macaroni and cheese with tuna. A banana peel hung off the rim of the metal trashcan.

Shaggy ignored the mess and made himself comfortable, pulling out a chair from the Goodwill-issue grey metal table. Adam excused himself to take a quick leak as Shaggy cracked open two of the beers. When he came back out, Shaggy handed him a can of Crest.

"Chug it, bro. You earned it!" They clinked cans together and each tried to down as much of the beer as they could in one gulp. Adam let out a huge belch, sat down next to Shaggy, and untied his shoes.

Shaggy extolled the virtues of Shauna's pussy, and told him the best way to prove it was to find out for himself. Adam smiled at the thought, already feeling drunk. He could stand to eat some pussy.

"Finish your brew, then you better wash all that blood off your leg, bro."

Adam polished off the remainder of his can and Shaggy did the same. Shaggy went to the fridge for two more. Adam stood and headed for the bathroom, wobbling slightly. He pulled the door shut behind him.

Adam stripped down and ran warm water in the tub. He stood in the bathtub and splashed water onto the back of his leg, clearing away the dried blood as gently as he could. Before long, it started to sting, and he pulled back. His knees trembled; the beer, blood loss, and steamed-up little room made him woozy. He sat on the edge of the tub to get his bearings and took stock of the evening. He'd conked a guy with a two-litre plastic bottle of Canada Dry. He'd stolen a purse. Now they were about to dope up a hooker? He was used to following Shaggy's lead, but maybe it was time to say something.

Adam scratched his forehead as he sat naked on the edge of the tub and drained a piss into it. He didn't know if he could have sex with someone as intimidating as Shauna, no matter what state she was in. He'd seen two guys and a woman in porn before and it wasn't too queer, but he didn't think he'd be able to pull it off. That single beer already made him so groggy. Couldn't they just go and score some coke? They probably had enough cash for half an eight-ball.

He'd better talk to Shag. Adam stood up and lost his balance, stumbling onto the toilet seat. He pulled the bathroom door open to let cooler air into the room, and struggled to put his underwear back on. Adam stepped out and found Shaggy in the kitchen counting out money from the studded change purse.

"Hey bro—another brew?"

Everything was slowing down on Adam, the blood dripping through his veins, his breathing, his numb footsteps. "Bud, I gotta rest a sec." Adam flopped onto his bed. As he leaned back, he caught a glimpse of the view outside. The sliver of a waxing crescent moon reflected in a puddle of motor oil in the back alley just beyond his window.

The last thing Adam remembered was the sensation of Shaggy's stubbly moustache brushing against his nose before their lips met and Shaggy's hand rubbing the hairs on his left leg, right above the knee. His touch was gentle, like that of a young girl tracing the spine of a kitten with her fingertip.

FAMILY
CIRCUS

I'M GOING TO TAKE THE KIDS away from all of this for good. Tomorrow. But for now, just get through tonight.

July 29. It's three a.m., and the apartment is full, rife with the gagging stench of nail-polish remover. The reek of Big Kathy's pungent Camels wafts in from the kitchen, mingling with the chemical haze rising from the aluminum baking trays. There's a tinge of mould in the air, too. And endless chitchat from the other girls in the apartment.

What's worse is I'm used to it—the dizzying odours, the absence of quiet. Sammy is too, and he's only eight. I put him in the living room. There's a door that shuts; he's probably still watching TV. I keep Cindy in the crib in the back bedroom when we wash the cheques, so the fumes don't get to her.

Still, I keep the place pretty clean. The crystal helps with that.

I know I need to get off it, but for now speed actually makes me a better mom. I manage to keep things tidy and focus on working the mail, and the money we get from that lets me feed the kids. Rent, meth, beer, food—in that order. And then clothes and toys for the kids. Oh, and formula for Cindy. I know it wouldn't be safe for her to take my breast milk. I'm not stupid.

In the kitchen, Big Kath opens the envelopes and extracts all the cheques, taking slugs of Carling Ice as if it were water, chain-smoking. As she sorts through the stolen mail, Kath makes piles. The largest one contains people's account information: bills and credit applications. Next to that, a stack of cheques. On the yellowed linoleum floor at her feet, everything else. The account numbers go to Rhonda, sitting at the computer in the front bedroom.

The cheques go to me. I soak them in acetone long enough for the ink to evaporate, then rewrite them in the name of Edna Windecker—an identity Rhonda created on the computer. "Edna" has a birth certificate, a health card, and driver's license. And an account at Crosstown; we figured a credit union would be lower profile. Rhonda told us she could make her a SIN card too. Zeke and I laughed at the thought. Why declare any income? Rhonda said if we had any sense we'd be buying RRSPs.

Zeke and Duarte are out on their last run of the night, boosting bags of garbage from behind the Osborne Street Cash Mart— they don't shred their paperwork there. The guys will throw it in the back of the red pickup and cover it with a tarp. They shouldn't be gone much longer.

Zeke will want to fuck when they get back. I hope we can shower first—everyone's got that ammonia drug smell leaking out their pores. I've never met anyone as horny as Zeke. I bet he's even fucked Duarte's round, hairy ass. He had to do something to keep himself busy when I was pregnant. Cindy's his. Sammy isn't.

Lise, the new girl, sits next to me. She's got a pretty face, I'll admit. Her skin's light brown and her hair is long and straight. Her upper lids are heavy with grey eye shadow. One of her front teeth is crooked. Zeke dropped her off with the last batch of mail, but it seemed like they already knew each other. A hooker from the corner of Furby and Ellice, I'm sure. Probably a glue sniffer. She wipes her runny nose with the back of her arm, blankly staring up at me.

When Zeke and I met two years ago, I would've been jealous at the thought of him with another woman. Now I'm relieved. All I can think of is the coming calm. Gimli is quiet, a town on the shore of Lake Winnipeg, with less than two thousand people. Sammy and Cindy will love it. I grew up there. Mom's there. She'll help me with the kids, especially seven-month-old Cindy. I'll need a while to sleep off all the meth—then we'll start over. I'll bring a baggie or two with me so I don't fall asleep at the wheel on the two-hour drive. After that, I'm done.

I quit tweaking when I was four months pregnant with Cindy, till a few weeks after she was born. Stopping was hard. She cried a lot at first, but she's okay now. I gave her a couple spoonfuls of cough syrup to make sure she'd sleep through tonight's freak show. Robitussin, my only reliable babysitter.

Lise's syringe sits on the coffee table in front of us. I've been snorting bumps instead of shooting up tonight. Gotta keep my wits about me for tomorrow. Once I cash the cheques in the morning—while everyone else is crashed out—I'm going to pick Sammy up from school at lunch, stop by here to get Cindy, then keep driving till we reach the water's edge.

Next to Lise's rig are three large aluminum baking trays from the Provencher IGA. The trays are full of acetone. That's where the cheques go. A small bottle of bleach sits on the shag rug next to the coffee table; it gets the ink that doesn't come out with the acetone. There's also a yellow chamois scrap and an ink eraser I sometimes use for touch-ups. I've gotten good at this.

"Get over here, motherfucker!" A shout from upstairs, followed by a woman's wordless shriek.

Fuck's sakes. It's that wrinkly weirdo in 13B and his drunk old bitch. One more reason to leave: I'm determined not to end up as pathetic as them. Maybe I'll be a doting old grandma by then. I hope no one calls 9-1-1 on them, not with everyone down here. I don't think he ever really hits her anyway. A heavy thump from above, and then nothing. Maybe I was wrong about that.

I get up, lurch toward the open window, and stick my head out toward the starless sky. On the street, a kid with a Mohawk revs by on a red motorbike. The tidy, yellow-brick façade of this building misleads: this is nothing but a slum. If you live here, you're either a struggling student, a whacked-out head case, a deadbeat on welfare, or some kind of crook.

I inhale through my nose, taking in as much clean night air as my lungs can hold. I wipe my brow and pull my fingers through my brittle hair. At least a half-inch of black roots have forced their way through my blonde dye job. When I get out of here, I'm going to grow it back out past my shoulders.

Anyway, back to teaching the new girl how to forge cheques. I turn toward the coffee table. Lise sits cross-legged like some gnarly hooker Buddha, injecting some of Zeke's speed into a vein in the sole of her foot. I wonder if she slams there for vanity's sake—her arms don't look so bad. As she pulls the needle out, Lise looks up at me, all brown almond eyes with big, vibrating pupils. Now that she's spun, maybe she'll pay better attention.

"That weird girl with the funny glasses came out of the bedroom. She looked rough." Lise means Rhonda, our hacker at the bedroom PC, with her vintage horn-rims. I could hear the sporadic clatter of her keyboard clicks from here. Rhonda's a bit kooky, yes, but her computer skills have come in handy. She works at Value Village; judging by her nerdy wardrobe, she obviously shops there too. She's a rapid-fire typist because she's high like the rest of us. Even over the chemical odours, I swear I can catch a whiff of her trademark BO-infused polyester scent. I may shoot up a lot, but at least I know how to bathe. Christ.

I sit down next to Lise and address her slowly. "I want you to pay attention now, okay?"

She stares in silence. She actually looks a bit frightened. I ask her age.

"Seventeen."

Oh boy. Anyway. "Take the piles of cheques and divide them

up by the type of ink. Anything felt-tip—like it was written with a small marker—put it in one pile. If it was done with a ball-point pen, make one pile for blue ink and one for black. Anything else weird, just put it in a separate pile. Got it?" I hand her the cheques and she begins to separate them. After a minute, she laughs and hands me one written in pencil.

"That should be easy enough to erase!"

"No. Pencil leaves trace marks grooved right into the paper. We've gotta throw those away." She drops it to the floor and continues sorting. Maybe she's not so dumb after all. I show her how to put the cheques in the wash one at a time using the tongs.

Sammy trudges into the living room, clad only in Underoos. Startled, I grab a newspaper and toss it on the coffee table, covering Lise's needle. He's carrying a tube of something. Toothpaste?

"What you got there, kiddo?"

"Cindy's got a sore in her mouth. It's called Orajel. I put it on the red spot when she wakes up crying. You didn't hear her, did you?"

Without waiting for an answer, he walks up to me, and I put my arms out, thinking he needs a hug. Instead, he unscrews the Orajel tube, puts some on his finger, and lightly touches my dry, chapped lip, smearing me gently with the numbing cream.

"Where'd you get that stuff, Sammy?"

"I asked Mrs Rainders." The next-door neighbour. He kisses my cheek and turns around. Passing Lise he pauses, reaching toward her trio of piles. He moves a mislaid blue-ink cheque from the black-ink pile to its proper place.

Sammy retreats to the living room and closes the door. Lise stares after him, smiling. "What a beautiful little boy."

A bump of crystal piled on the tip of my house key, I hold it up to my nostril and snort back hard. After the initial bite of pain as the shards hit my nasal membranes, warmth spreads from my face through the rest of my body. I hadn't heard Cindy cry with all the racket. I oughta check on her more.

"I had a baby girl once," Lise says with a distracted look. "When I was fifteen. But they came and took her away."

"Who?"

"Winnipeg Child and Family Services. They gave her away to a white family."

I thought she'd looked kinda Native. Métis, maybe?

"My mom called them on me. I wasn't even living at home anymore. She heard about the baby from my sister."

Rhonda steps out of the bedroom wearing only a pair of panties, waving a trembling hand in front of her face. Her body's slick with perspiration. "The FTP server cacked out again." She stumbles on her feet, sweat running off her face and breasts, dripping onto the carpet by the cupful.

I yell into the kitchen, "Kath!"

Big Kath gets up from her chair, lifts Rhonda like she's a toothpick, and efficiently transports her to the bathroom. I watch her nude form shake as she babbles in the older woman's muscular grasp. "Am I gonna die?" she sputters.

Christ, not again. Stupid bitch. I step behind them, look Rhonda in the face, and say in a loud voice, "You're not going to die, honey." Kath will make sure she cools down and doesn't drown or convulse. We've been through this twice before with Rhonda.

Lise carefully lays out washed cheques on the paper towels next to the trays. She looks closely at one of them and puts it back in the wash. I'm impressed. There's a light thud from the bathroom, then the sound of the running shower. The phone rings. Zeke sounds wired. "I'm coming home."

"You got mail?"

"Yeah, I almost lost Duarte though."

"What?"

"He was taking a piss behind the Cash Money on Portage. Standing at the dumpster with his rod hanging out, a bag of their garbage on either side of him when this blond Nazi cop shows up. Duarte talked his way out of it, but we took the long way home in case they were tailing us." Paranoid as usual. I can't wait to get away from him.

"We're coming home," Zeke repeats himself. "Got lots of stuff. Everyone still working?"

"Rhonda's having an OD in the bathroom. Kath's taking care of it."

"Good. Lise there?"

"Yeah."

"See you in ten."

I hang up and head back to the can, hoping Rhonda hasn't turned blue. She's sitting naked in the shower, head lolling to one side. Hosed down, she still smells. "She's asleep," Kath tells me, washing her hands in the sink.

"Thank fuck."

The apartment door rattles and pushes inward. Zeke and Duarte barge in with goofy grins on their faces. At six-five, fair-haired Zeke has to duck his head to get through the door. Swarthy, bearded Duarte is shorter than me. They each lug big garbage bags in both hands.

"It's Christmas, kids!" Zeke drops the bags off in the kitchen, giving Big Kath that three-part macho handshake I've never been able to get straight.

"Ho ho ho!" spouts Duarte, slamming the door with his foot. They must be drunk and high. Zeke heads my way.

"C'mere, baby," he says. Is he talking to me or Lise?

I never find out because he doesn't make it across the room. The front door—which the guys didn't lock behind them—slams on its hinges, kicked open. Two police officers: a short, black woman and a tall, blond male.

"No one move!" the man bellows.

"Fuck—not you!"

In a minute they've got both the guys on the ground. The male cop bellows at me and Lise. "Back on the couch. Sit down and shut up!"

"Shit—the kids!" Whispered through clenched teeth.

Lise grabs my hand and squeezes. "I'll protect them," she hisses, slipping toward the back of the apartment. The cops, subduing Zeke and Duarte, don't notice.

The black officer leans down and twists Duarte's arm behind his back. "Lay off, cunt!" Duarte shouts.

She pulls out her nightstick and gives Duarte's ass crack a vicious thwack, then smiles. He shuts up. She leans down in his face, all teeth. "Like that, you greasy, fucking faggot?" Duarte mutters in Spanish. She puts him in handcuffs to match Zeke's and kicks him in the side.

Sammy runs into the room, followed by Lise. She tries to scoop him up in her arms, but trips and falls instead, banging her forehead on the edge of the coffee table. She's down. I watch as she starts to bleed from the head. Sammy lunges forward.

"Baby, stop!" He ignores me and heads right for the male officer. Before the cop can react, Sammy reaches up and slams him in the nuts with his fist. With a surprised, angry yelp, he grabs his groin. Sammy throws his arms around the cop's right leg and bites into his flank through the dark blue pants. "Jesus, fuck!"

His partner reaches over and yanks Sammy by the shoulders, pulling him off and holding him in the air, away from her body. He continues to kick and yell. "If you send my mom to jail, I'll fucking kick your fucking asses!"

She puts Sammy face down on the floor between Zeke and Duarte. The male officer steps forward and stomps his foot onto Sammy's back, immobilizing him. He keeps yelling. The officer kicks his kidneys. Sammy shuts down, but I can see his body heaving like he's going to hyperventilate. I feel numb.

The female cop, weapon drawn, heads back to scope out the rest of the apartment. Lise rouses on the floor, wipes her bloody face, and crawls over to join me at the couch. Rhonda walks into the room, head down, and sits next to us. The tip of Lise's syringe pokes out from underneath a pile of cheques on the coffee table. Rhonda can't take her eyes off it.

Big Kath sits in the kitchen and fixes the male officer with a surly stare, her large hands trembling in her lap. He surveys the contents of the kitchen table. Next to a stack of cheques sit a half-dozen baggies of speed. Putting on a latex glove, he slips the drugs into an evidence bag.

Lise leans in toward me. "Cindy is safe," she whispers.

I stare at her, uncomprehending.

"I hid her in the laundry hamper. They won't find her." She grabs my hand. "I put all her blankets on top of her. They'll never find her. She'll be safe."

The female officer's voice calls out from the back bedroom. "Jackson, call an ambulance. Now!"

The psych ward at Johnson Memorial isn't quite by the water's edge, but I can still see Lake Winnipeg from my room. I've slept through the past three weeks.

I could say a bunch of other stuff, but fuck it. Mom told me everything. Cindy stopped breathing but was revived. She's in the hospital back in the city. Zeke and Duarte went to jail. Sammy's in a foster home. Mom said she'd look into adopting Sammy and Cindy. I told her don't bother. They're better off with someone else. After all, I did what I planned to. I got them out of there.

SNAP

THE GLOWING TUBE IN THE FIXTURE above Jake's head bathed his cubicle in a green-tinged hue. Fluorescents wouldn't be so bad except for the intermittent buzzing noises they emitted. The same moment the phone rang, the light flickered for a few seconds. Ghostly intervention or electronic glitch—he didn't know which, but he was used to it by now. Jake reached over and picked it up after the second ring.

"Social Services, Jake Wharton." Gruff, tired.

"Oh, hey, babe," he said. Relieved, smiling. It was Lara. He glanced over a precarious pile of green file folders toward a framed photo of the two of them, taken last year at Canada's Wonderland. Like the rest of the items on his desk, the picture needed to be dusted.

She wanted to know if he was up for drinks over at their next-door neighbours' after tonight's meeting. Jake thought it best to decline.

"A new guy in group is turning out to be a real asshole." These meetings were draining; Jake often came out of them depressed and moody. He liked their neighbours, Fausto and Reg, well enough; they were the first male couple he'd really gotten to know, but later tonight he might not be the best company.

"You go ahead. I'll probably hit the sack early. It's been a week." He promised to keep the bed warm for her, then ended the call. With him out of the picture, maybe they'd end up at that male peeler bar again. Jake found the idea of male strippers hard to comprehend. He couldn't imagine himself on a stage jiggling his buttocks, he knew that much. He didn't even especially care to watch women do it either.

It was five-thirty. In another hour, his weekly counselling session with the sex-offenders group. Some Friday night.

Jake surveyed his desk: an inbox stacked with papers imprinted with letters like swarms of tiny black ants. Every stapled set of sheets required a piece of him in some form or another; casework needed updating or sorting—echoes of people's pain converted into tidy reportage and shovelled back into musty folders. Each one bore a man's name written with a black Sharpie. Because therapy wasn't equally successful with all offenders, some files were much thicker than others. Half the crap on paper also had to be typed into the fucking computer. Jake hated it.

He wasn't looking forward to tonight's session, thanks to Steve Woodruff, whose folder sat at the top of the pile. Three years ago, Steve anally raped a woman he'd met at a nightclub.

Snap

It had been his first offence—as far as the authorities knew. Just out of jail, tonight would be Steve's third session of court-mandated group therapy. He delighted in riling and antagonizing the others. At his first session, he seemed drunk. The next week, he issued a racial slur to the man sitting next to him and later made a lewd comment about another man's daughter, almost causing a pair of fist fights. Jake had fought the urge to punch Steve's face himself, to wipe away his perpetual smirk.

Over Jake's head, the fluorescent flickered again. He ran his fingers through his long black hair. Jake felt older than thirty-three. He'd been running the sex-offenders group for three years, but it felt much longer. Before Steve's arrival, the group had finally reached a certain level of serenity—as much as that was possible among a gang of eight men whose sole common denominator was the fact that they'd sexually forced themselves on others.

He'd dealt with jackasses before—the nature of the job—but Jake felt ground down tonight. Hoped he had it in him to wrangle with this dick Steve, to defuse him somehow. The guy possessed a sly, devious intelligence—and disruptions like his could have a poisonous effect on the rest of the group. A few guys had been in the program for two years, had not re-offended, and were ready to graduate. *I don't want anyone to screw this up for them*, Jake thought. He wondered if he should consider returning to his previous field of expertise, crisis counselling for suicidal youth. Or maybe he just needed a vacation—some place quiet, where no one had any problems.

The joys of social work. At least he wasn't involved in the initial intake work for sexual offenders in the therapy program. That involved confirmation of their attraction to sexual violence or underage victims by placing a ringed device at the base of the men's penises and measuring the flow of blood to their members while showing them snuff images and kiddie porn and playing them audio tapes of women screaming or the voices of young children. Yes, his job could be worse.

But they were successful at least part of the time; had the stats to prove it. He'd seen more than one profound transformation—and more than one lapse with tragic consequences. Some days he was moved by the thought of helping people change for the better. Other days, it was just a job. And a really draining one at that.

"How do you think it made your daughter feel when she was alone with you, and you touched her where you did?" Jake posed his question to Roger Collins, who sat across from him in the semi-circle of folding chairs in the basement of the Catholic church. Jake affected an inquisitive but neutral tone. "Try to put yourself in her shoes," he added, prodding Roger. The thirty-something fidgeted in his metal folding chair, causing it to creak. He opened and closed his mouth, pushing stringy black hair over a sweating forehead and adjusting thick, black-framed glasses. Roger had spent three years genitally fondling his daughter, who was now twelve. He ceased once she'd started to menstruate—and confided in her gym teacher after starting to cry in the middle of her first sex-ed class.

Roger was tentative. "I love Sarah. She's still my little baby," he said. "I never actually hurt her. I thought we could make each other feel good in a way that wasn't…" He paused. "Complicated."

"But Roger, Sarah missed the rest of the school year. She may not have said anything at the time, but that doesn't mean that you didn't hurt her or violate her trust. Wouldn't you agree?" Though Roger had made progress in individual therapy and was no longer denying what he'd done, this was the first time he'd spoken up in group.

The bespectacled man stayed stock still, completely mum. Over in a corner, Jake's boss Herschel Weiss scratched his beard and made a few scribbles in his notepad. Herschel sat in on counselling sessions at least once a month, sometimes accompanied by a parole officer or the woman from the victim advocate office. Most of the men were used to speaking about their actions in front of others; according to the dictates of the program, eschewing secrecy was an important part of the treatment process.

Sitting next to Jake, Desmond Jones spoke up. A very tall man with dreadlocks tucked inside a black woolen tam, he cut an imposing figure even when seated. In contrast to Roger's stuttering chirp, Desmond's deep voice was measured.

"Roger, you weren't even thinking about how your child felt. When you hurt her, you were only thinking of yourself. Like you were on a train headed straight for her, like she was tied up on the track. What you need to learn now"—he paused to cock his head at Roger and smile—"is how to stop the train before it's too late."

It was hard to believe Desmond was only twenty-two. His calm demeanour made him seem like the "gentle giant" of the group. But Jake was sure that in Desmond's past that same quiet self-assurance and magnetic personality had been used to win the confidence of young boys. Desmond and Roger were the only two child abusers in the group; the other six men preyed on adults. Jake was pretty confident about Desmond's future; for Roger, however, the jury was still out.

Roger looked Desmond in the eye and sparked a thin smile before looking down at the floor and sinking into his chair. Then Steve Woodruff turned abruptly toward him, his posture electric. Steve was lean with blond hair and a very trim beard; his blue eyes narrowed, making them seem almost black.

"I know what it feels like to get fucked," Steve spat at Roger. "It hurts. You bleed. How can you pretend that it didn't hurt your daughter? Did she ask for that? Fuck no, you pig. Just how disgusting are you?" He stared Roger down, poised spring-like on his seat's edge.

Roger sputtered. "I…I…I…never did that to her!"

"But you would have started to soon if she hadn't ratted you out—and you'll always be waiting for your chance now, right?" Steve let the suggestion hover in the air. "You'll never change," he pronounced, looking away from the group and toward the black wooden door that marked the room's exit. From around the circle of seated men there were grunts of agreement.

Roger sank back further into his chair, crumpling into himself.

Jake's professional calm disappeared. "And Steve, how do you think the woman you assaulted felt while *you* were violating her?" he asked pointedly.

"Not as bad as when it happened to me," Steve snarled in retort. According to his file, there was no history of sexual abuse in his own childhood—but Steve had claimed during his intake assessment that he'd been raped in prison by a gang of men. Steve looked Jake directly in the eye, his facial expression somewhere between a self-satisfied smile and a confrontational leer.

"She had a nervous breakdown, Steve. She had tremors and diarrhea for a year straight. You took something away from her, *Steve,* and you didn't even know her name." Jake's face was bright red. In the far corner of the room, Herschel stared.

Steve's eyes never left Jake's. "Her name was Liz, Jake. And your wife's name is Lara." Steve smiled, then looked around the room at the other men in the circle.

Jake was startled into a moment of silence, after which he brought the meeting to a close. He left the room, and the other men quickly followed suit, a few of them pulling cigarette packs out of their pockets as they climbed the stairs.

Minutes later, Herschel barged into the men's room, where Jake stood at a urinal relieving himself. The dimly lit basement restroom was old and grimy. Dank and musty, the air was filled with the scent of urine-splashed mothballs.

"Jake, what the fuck was that? You know how to do this. If your temper ever comes into play, you've lost control. You were right to confront someone who tries to deny his culpability, but you have to do it *calmly.*"

More social-worker bullshit. I hate this crap, Jake thought. He shook off, zipped up, and then walked over to wash his hands in the yellow, cracked sink.

"I'll keep it in check."

"You better, Jake. I had confidence in you when you first took over the group, but I don't know what's up with you lately."

"Did you hear how he brought up Lara? He also mentioned he knew I live in Little Italy during our one-on-one last week. He's trying to spook me."

"Jake, there are ways to deal with intimidation tactics—rational ways. You know this," Herschel replied. "I'm worried you might need to take a bit of a break. I've talked with Maureen Dixon about it." Herschel's supervisor, the district manager.

Jake was silent.

"We'll talk again Monday morning. First thing. Got it?" Herschel left the washroom and Jake heard footsteps recede as his boss walked down the hall and ascended the staircase.

The carpaccio was moist and salty. "You gotta try this," Jake said, pushing the appetizer plate in Lara's direction. He watched as she speared a slice of the meat with her fork and brought it to her lips. "Tasty," she concurred with a nod and a smile, helping herself to another piece.

Jake thought Lara was more beautiful now than she was when they had met six years ago. Curly red hair framed her lightly freckled skin, and her face was graced with expressive, thoughtful eyes. Behind her, just beyond Marinella's sidewalk patio, the springtime lunch-hour bustle of their neighbourhood was on parade. An old Italian man shuffled along the street with slow determination, propelled forward by a hand-carved wooden cane. A plaid-jacketed kid with a fauxhawk and an iPod manoeuvred past him with a look of impatience on her face.

Jake's nostrils widened at the earthy smell of the wild mushroom risotto that sat in front of him, its steam rising into his face. Caught up in his surroundings, he hadn't even noticed when their entrées had arrived. The service here was discreet and efficient; he looked down and saw his wine glass had also been filled.

A quiet day hanging around the house yesterday had done wonders for his mood. They had slept in, done the *Toronto Star* crossword in bed together, and then sat on the front porch during an unexpected rainstorm. For the first time in ages he'd been able to relax.

Lara waved in his face to pull him out of his reverie. "If you're sure you don't want to come this time, I'll probably sleep over at Dad's. He'll want to stay up late playing cards, I'm sure. I'm off tomorrow anyway." She worked four days a week as a literacy educator at a community centre and always had Mondays off.

Lara saw her dad in Guelph for dinner every other Sunday. A rough-hewn man who'd spent forty years working at a refrigerator and freezer plant before retiring last year, he had raised Lara on his own—with some help from his own mother and two sisters—after Mrs Biscombe was killed by a drunk driver when Lara was eight. He was fiercely protective of Lara, and she was devoted to him as well. Thinking back to his work for the first time all weekend, Jake wished all fathers and daughters could have the sort of relationship that Lara had with her dad. Although Mike had been suspicious of Jake at first—accusing him of being a biker because he wore his hair long—he eventually warmed to his son-in-law.

"Give your dad a hug for me," he said, reaching over to steal a bite of her lasagna. When Lara spoke, her quiet voice was nearly drowned out by a honking horn followed by the clank of the bell on the passing streetcar.

"Have you thought any more about the trip to Cuba?" On Friday night, Fausto and Reg had talked to her about their planned vacation in Havana. They wanted to see the historic city before Castro's death. "Obama's gonna swoop in and change everything," Reg had declared. Fausto spoke Italian and thought he could fake his way through enough Spanish for them to move beyond the usual tourist sites and see the "real" Havana. Jake thought Fausto's conception of the trip was overly ambitious but had to admit he never would have thought of doing this himself. Lara seemed to feed off the couple's energy and stimulation. They both always seemed inspired—and in contrast, Jake felt flat.

"Could be a good idea," he told her. "I'll have a talk with Reg about it later tonight." Reg was the more stoic of the two men, and he was a social worker too. Jake had always found that he could relate to him better than Fausto.

"You should give them a call tonight. Or call Jorge and go see a movie or something."

Jake agreed that he'd find a way to occupy himself for the evening. "I haven't hung with Jorge in weeks," he conceded.

He still hadn't mentioned Steve's outburst or his talk with Herschel—he didn't want to worry her, and he was trying not to think about it. But he knew she could sense things weren't getting any better at work. She just didn't know he might end up with lots of time for a vacation whether he liked it or not.

Lara went inside to use the washroom while Jake put the bill on his Visa. Downing the last swallow of his now-lukewarm latte, he glanced out to the street. In the Starbucks directly across the road, Steve Woodruff sat in the front window staring back at him. In one hand he held a Frappuccino; in the other, a cell phone. As Lara came back outside to join him, Jake felt his BlackBerry vibrate in his pants pocket.

His insides turned cold, but Jake did not acknowledge the pulsing as it repeated against his thigh. He held Lara's hand as they walked down College Street, not looking back. When they stopped at the corner traffic light, he reached into his pocket with his other hand and discreetly held down the top button to put the device into sleep mode.

Jake saw Lara off at the train station, kissing her goodbye, and watched as the green commuter train pulled out, its oddly shaped cars like bullets travelling in slow motion. He spent the next hour walking home slowly. His eyes focused on the sidewalk as he moved north on University Avenue, the mid-afternoon sun bearing down on his shoulders. Nearing College Street, his eyes drew upward as he approached the Hydro building, a rectangular monolith whose entire surface was comprised of giant sheets of mirrored glass. Its faceless architecture chilled him, and he cast his eyes downward again as he rounded the corner.

Forty minutes later, Jake entered the side door of their house and made his way to the bedroom. He doffed his sweat-soaked clothes and put on a pair of PJs to lounge in. He then reached into the pocket of his jeans and took out his BlackBerry. A single message waited. He retrieved it.

"What, you never call me anymore?" a boisterous, Portuguese-accented voice called into his ear. It was Jorge, his bud from the pool hall up the street. "I ran into Lara at the grocery last Monday, she said I oughta give you a call this weekend." Jake saved the message without listening to the rest of it and decided not to return the call. Despite his promise to Lara, he didn't speak to anyone else for the rest of the day, choosing instead the more low-key company of a couple of cans of Pabst and reruns of *Quincy, M.E.* and *Columbo* on the oldies cable channel. He went to bed early for the third night in a row. Sleep came quickly.

After hours of slumber, Jake found himself slowly roused by sensations of pleasure—a low flame that started in his testes and pulled upward, buzzing warmly through his groin as he lay on his back. Through lazy eyelids, he gazed upon Lara, naked, as she slid onto his erect shaft and enveloped him within her. Still in a fog of sleep, he smiled like a drunk. Lara leaned forward and started to grind her hips up and down, taking him inside her more deeply. Her small breasts swayed. He could smell her, and it made him harder. She smiled as he began to strain inside her, then raised her head upward, closing her eyes and slowly running her index and middle fingers along either side of her wet exposed clit. But when she looked back down, the smile had turned into a mean sneer. Continuing to move up and down against him, Lara started to snort with disgust. Her laughter grew until it filled the room, mocking him. Jake felt confusion and shame. As she pointed at his face and shrieked even louder, he swiftly raised his left fist and struck her hard. He felt and heard the cartilage in her nose snap as his knuckles connected with her face.

Lara leaned forward, then froze, a glazed look of mute shock spreading across her face. Both her nostrils instantly reddened; blood began to spurt from her nose in a quickening drip. The red liquid poured out of each nostril, conjoining in a single stream that poured directly onto the thick black hairs of Jake's chest, matting them like oil paint.

Jake trembled as he lay on his side and began to weep in silence. He had never raised a hand to Lara in real life—he rarely even raised his voice to her. He couldn't imagine hurting her physically—but this wasn't the first time he'd had this puzzling dream. One thing was different this time—the look on her face before she began to howl in laughter. It was identical to the hateful leer he'd seen on Steve Woodruff's face. Tears trickled from his left eye over his nose and dripped onto the sheet, and he began to shake his head and rock his body from side to side, now sobbing aloud. He realized he was completely alone, and it didn't matter how much noise he made.

His heart pounded in his ears, and he felt like he might lose control of his bowels. Jake cried until his face and throat hurt, then picked up the phone to call in sick. Talking to rapists was just not an option today. In fact, he wondered if he could ever do it again.

After sleeping in late, Jake brewed a pot of organic coffee. For the time being, he tried not to think about work—he knew he'd have some explaining to do with Herschel, and he wasn't completely sure what to say. Never mind the question of his future at the agency, but he'd also be missing half of his one-on-one sessions with the offenders, which were scheduled for today and tomorrow.

Sitting at the wooden kitchen table Lara's dad had made, he let his mind wander and allowed the nutty aroma wafting up from his mug to tweak his nostrils awake. Through the window into the backyard, he saw his neighbour Fausto crouched down in the yard next door. Tying the sash on his navy housecoat, Jake got up and went outside. As he approached, he could see sweat glistening atop the large man's balding head.

Fausto was a freelance editor with a flexible schedule, which allowed him to pick the tomatoes in his garden whenever he pleased. He placed the ripe, red one in his hand into a wooden basket next to him. Wiping his hand on an oversized orange T-shirt, he stood up to shake Jake's hand.

"How's it going, Jake?"

"I've been better. Taking a mental-health day. Work's been getting me down."

"Yeah, I've gotten that sense. You need a job like mine. My biggest client is a law firm that specializes in homeless clients. I help people, but without getting my hands dirty, sitting alone in my den." A smile crossed his round face.

Jake changed the subject. "Lara says you've been doing a lot of planning for this Cuba trip."

"Well, I've been spending more non-billable hours than I should looking up information on Havana online. Did you know there's more than one Havana?"

Jake gave him a quizzical look.

"You learn these things when you do Internet research," Fausto continued, warming to his subject. "As one might suspect, there's a city in Florida named after Cuba's capital. But the one that surprised me was Havana, Arkansas."

Jake smirked in surprise, wondering if there might also be a Havana, PEI, as well.

"There are 392 people in Havana, Arkansas—and not one of them is black. In the heart of the Deep South. I'm not sure how safe we'd be visiting there."

Jake wasn't sure if Fausto was referring to being gay—or the fact that his partner Reg was of African descent. He simply nodded. He wasn't sure what to say next, but was rescued by a loud rapping that sounded like it was coming from his own front door.

"Got to run, big guy. Talk to you again soon."

Jake re-entered the house and headed toward the front door. He stepped out onto the front porch. Steve Woodruff sat a few feet away in Lara's wicker chair.

Steve stood, seeming woozy and unsteady on his feet. "You sure walk slow," he said. Jake noticed a few splotches of blood at the bottom of Steve's untucked shirt and the front of his corduroy pants. One splotch was shaped like a kidney.

Jake stared at him wordlessly, as the smell of liquor wafted toward him. He twitched, his face reddening with anger.

"I followed you home from the train station yesterday," Steve explained. "Didn't think you'd ever get here. I'm a sneaky bastard, huh?"

"Why are you here, Steve?"

Steve made a show of looking at his watch. "I didn't want to be late for my eleven o'clock." He hiccupped, then belched. "You told us that we're never going to get better if we don't get responsible, remember?" The drunk raised one exaggerated eyebrow like a sideshow mime, then burst out laughing.

Jake waited for Steve's manic snicker to subside. Then he spoke in a tranquil tone, as if counselling a man standing on a skyscraper's windowsill to come back inside. Except that he felt as if he were the man on the ledge.

"Steve, you don't have to report in today. I called in sick. Didn't Genevieve call to let you know? She'll reschedule you for later in the week. Nothing to worry about."

"I haven't been home all morning. And I wasn't at my shit job either." Steve responded to the kinder-sounding fake Jake by affecting a sing-sing tone in his own voice: "Not at home, not at work! Nowhere to be found!" He listed forward for a moment before recapturing his balance. Steve stared into Jake's eyes without blinking, then spoke again.

"I followed Roger home Friday night after group." Steve put one hand into his pants pocket. "And I went to visit the fucking pedophile creep this morning too."

Steve's tone hardened. "I wanted him to know what it feels like…Didn't want to deal with his screams, so I hit him on the head first. With this," he said, pulling a short black revolver from his pocket. *You dirty fucking faggot rapist,* Jake thought reflexively, all his sensitivity training out the window. He gazed at Steve as neutrally as he could manage and waited.

Steve held the weapon up by the barrel rather than aiming it. With his other hand, he gestured toward the handle. "See, no blood. I only hit him hard enough to knock him out." he said. "'This one's for little Sarah,' I told him."

Steve continued to stare at the revolver in his hand as if dazzled by it until he was interrupted by a voice from behind him. Lara stood there on the porch steps.

"Steve, what are *you* doing here?" she asked.

Jake and Steve both said her name at the same time.

"Lara," Steve repeated. "I'm going back to jail." Steve lowered the gun to his side. His body quivered in a drunken crying jag. Lara stared at him in silence.

"I need to go back in," he said to her with finality. "Help me?"

He dropped the gun. It hit the grey-painted planks of the floor with a heavy thud but did not go off. Steve stretched his arms out to Lara. She approached Steve and placed one arm around his sodden, convulsing frame. After a long minute, she sat him down in a chair. Lara took her cell out of her pocket and phoned 9-1-1.

The cop car had pulled away a few minutes earlier. Jake recounted Steve's confession to the officers, and one of them sent an ambulance to pick up Roger Collins and take him to the hospital. "Roger had been making a lot of progress before now," Jake told the officers. Neither seemed interested.

Lara stepped back onto the front porch. She sat next to Jake on the steps, setting a red knapsack down beside her. He took her hand, solid where his was limp.

"How do you know Steve Woodruff?" he asked her.

"He bags groceries at the No Frills. I had no idea he was one of your clients." She paused. "I've talked to him while cashing out a few times. He seemed really sweet."

Jake turned away.

"He asked me out on a date."

"That scumbag. What did you say?"

"It was nice to get the attention."

Jake squeezed Lara's hand and then stroked her cheek. "Lara, Hersch wants me to take some time off. Do you still want to take that trip to—"

"We need time apart." She faced him. "We're going through the motions—and you haven't even noticed." Jake was unresponsive.

"I'm going back to Dad's. I've taken the rest of the week off work. Call you after that." Picking up her knapsack, she stepped off the porch and walked away.

Jake watched as Laura moved down the street and out of sight. He got up, went in the house, walked into the bedroom, and closed the door. He removed his clothes and lay on the bed. "Fuck," he said, and waited for the tears to come.

GET BRENDA FOXWORTHY

I GOT OFF THE BLUE NIAGARA TRANSIT BUS and crossed the road, entering the yard behind Simcoe Street Public School. Walking alone at night put me on edge. The schoolyard was empty, and I felt so nervous.

God fucking damn it. Rickie told me she'd be here a half-hour ago. Leaning against the fence, I pinched my arm as punishment for swearing, though I hadn't even said it out loud. Tapped out a nervous rhythm on the pile of dusty pebbles under my discount-store sneaker. Sweat broke out on my brow, courtesy of the late summer humidity weighing down the air, even in early evening. Wiped my forehead with the back of my hand. Tonight, we were going to do something outrageous, like nothing I'd ever dared before.

The three of us agreed to meet behind the elementary school, to draw as little attention as possible. Where could be quieter than the backyard of a grade school in August, especially this late at night? We all worked at the Village, but Preet had the night free to take his mom and dad to a temple in St. Catharines for some Hindu holiday. Rickie's shift ended at nine o'clock, and she promised she'd hurry over. Preet would pick us up before ten, as soon as he was back in Niagara Falls. I thought about where we were going: Brenda Foxworthy's house. There wasn't sufficient skin on both my arms to pinch myself enough times for all the swearing that nasty girl's name inspired in me. For once I wanted to do more than just swear.

I was off work because Ed hadn't scheduled me any shifts at all that weekend. What a prick. I pinched my arm again, wishing my boss wasn't so good-looking. Ed managed us parking-lot attendants at Maple Leaf Village amusement park every summer. Nineteen and a typical macho jock, he was in the law-and-security program at Niagara College. You got the feeling he liked being in charge. He also liked to wear tight shirts that showed off his arms and chest, both of which possessed wiry spirals of manly hair. When he wasn't ruling the roost at work, I would see him trolling around Clifton Hill in his white Trans Am. Checking out the chicks, I guessed. He was ridiculously proud of that stupid car and bragged to all the guys at work about it.

I was pissed about the time off. I needed that summer job. Not all of us have rich dads to pay for school clothes, let alone shiny white cars. When he saw me looking at the schedule in the office yesterday, Ed came up to me with a fake-looking smile and patted me on the shoulder. "Sorry about that, buddy. Too many guys on the team this year, I can't fit everybody in every single weekend."

His firm hand on my shoulder had caused some stirring in my underwear, but I willed my groin back under control. What a phony. Ed was not my "buddy" at all. One time, when he and I were alone in the office and I complained about having to work late, he actually put me into a headlock with my face in his armpit till I said "uncle." I remembered the smell—and the shame. The scent I secretly liked, the feeling of defeat I sure didn't. I never told anyone. Ed had pet names for all the parking guys; to my face, he called me Supermodel because I'm thin. I knew he called me "Dean the Queen" behind my back. Then again, who didn't? Preet and Rickie, that's who.

If there's one thing the three of us never spoke about, it was anything related to sex. Maybe that made us atypical eleventh graders, but for each of us the topic was a sore spot. Rickie was a loner who only had male friends. She and Preet played basketball together. "Rick's just one of the guys," Preet had explained once. "I basically treat her a hundred percent like a bro—the only thing we don't do alike is use the same washroom." I'd never seen her use a bathroom at all, in fact.

I'd been friends with Preet since grade eight, when his family moved to Canada. Mrs McDowell, my homeroom teacher, asked me to befriend him when he first arrived and spoke only Punjabi. Over time, he became well-liked—Preet was smart, friendly, great at sports, and very handsome. He was able to run in the popular circles at school, with friends on both the football team and student council. But he kept most of those people at arms' length, maintaining a close friendship with me, even as the others christened me "queer of the year."

I'd known Rickie even longer. One day, when I was in grade five, she started to follow me home and threatened to beat the shit out of me for calling her adopted brother a chink. She'd gotten bad information. Her brother was a tough little kid—there was no way I'd have provoked him, even though he was two years younger than me. And, of course, I'd have never said that word; I pinched myself again just thinking it. It wasn't the first time someone chased me home or beat me up, and it certainly hadn't been the last. But I had both Preet and Rickie to watch my back now, which was a relief. Would I ever stand up for myself? Yes, I thought. Tonight.

A screech of tires a block away tore me from my thoughts. A sleek black car gunned up Armory Street like a drag racer, though there was not another vehicle in sight to compete with. Instinctively I drew closer to the fence. As the car passed, I heard a guy on the passenger side laugh as he tossed a crumpled Coke can out the window at me. The car skidded to a halt at Victoria Avenue, then quickly pulled around the corner and out of sight, a chorus of yelping neighbourhood dogs barking in its wake. Soon all was quiet again.

Blocks away, tourist trap Clifton Hill was loaded with noisy idiots: loud American visitors buying cotton candy for kids up well past their normal bedtimes, drunks from around the world stumbling down the street in search of a greasy burger, honeymooners destined for heart-shaped hot tubs, and a few late-night sightseers at the foot of the hill arguing about which Niagara waterfall was the best. What a bunch of losers. I yawned just thinking about it.

"Hey, Dean." Her low, gravelly voice came out of nowhere. I jumped and actually shrieked a little. Rickie had walked through the schoolyard instead of up the street, surprising me from behind.

"Thank God you're here. You scared me!" I put my hand on my chest, and my body shook, all nerves.

Towering over me by three inches, she put a reassuring hand on my shoulder. With her short, dark crew-cut and bulky build, Rickie looked like a football player. In my mind, the high-school football team set the bar in terms of masculinity—and I always fell short. With her strong, self-assured demeanour, Rickie had it down without even trying. But while just thinking about those guys filled me with anxiety, Rickie's presence had a calming effect. I turned to her and smiled.

"How was work?"

"The usual."

"Anyone barf?"

"Nope, believe it or not."

"Anyone jump?"

"Hey, that's not funny, kid." She grabbed me playfully by the scruff of the neck. She was always calling me "kid" even though we were both sixteen. Her father used the same expression all the time. A single dad, he was a mechanic at Niagara Falls Auto.

Rickie operated the giant Ferris wheel at Maple Leaf Village. It was 200 feet tall. Someone tried to jump from it once this summer. Rickie hadn't been working that day, so I don't know why she was acting so sensitive about it. The guy didn't actually die.

I paused before my next question. "Did you see Brenda?"

Rickie's eyes locked with mine. "She's still there." Her voice cut like glass. In three short, sharp shards, you could hear exactly how Rickie felt about Brenda.

I had no idea why Brenda Foxworthy even had a job. Her father was an alderman and her mother a real-estate agent. Still, she worked at the Village like the rest of us Niagara teens. She sold fudge to tourists in a booth where she dressed in a uniform with a short white skirt. What a princess. What a bitch. I didn't bother to pinch myself for swearing anymore. Brenda was still at work. Good. Everything was going according to plan. Now if only Preet would get here.

Rickie carried the rope in a brown paper bag. Preet was bringing the metal hook. In my knapsack, I had the long, sharp knife.

The three of us lived within blocks of one another, we all worked on the same gaudy tourist strip, and we ended up in most of the same high-school classes. But right now what bound us together was our intense hatred for Brenda. Rickie and I turned when we heard the low rumble of an automobile engine. It was Preet, approaching slowly in his brother Vijay's black Mercury.

The car pulled up, and we got inside.

"Hey, how's it going?" Preet called out over the car stereo as Rickie took the front seat and I got into the back. He shook hands with both of us. Preet usually did that; it was one of his macho behaviours that, to me, felt both alien and adorable at the same time. As we passed all the drunken yahoos outside the Caverly Tavern, Preet rolled up the windows and turned on the air conditioning. "Shit, it's a hot night."

We made nervous small talk as we drove to our destination—Brenda's expansive house in the city's tony north end, Stamford Centre. I kept quiet—because Preet's taste in music drove me crazy. I hated ZZ Top.

Why couldn't he have the Jane Siberry cassette instead? Preet told us how they barely made it to the temple because both his brothers had come home drunk and started an argument with his father.

We all had our own reasons for what we were about to do. Why did I hate Brenda Foxworthy? Well, for years I'd disliked her as much as the other rich posers who made up the gifted program at our school. I was supposedly smarter than average, but I always felt like a fish out of water in that group—most of whom had been "gifted" since birth: gifted with violin lessons and trips to Europe, granted anything they ever wanted. I'd always been a wallflower in that program until last year when we got involved in the Board of Ed's problem-solving competition. We were put into teams to strategize solutions to social issues like acid rain. I was surprised how much I enjoyed our preparatory sessions, which involved both creative thinking and stuff that I actually cared about. For once, I felt motivated in my otherwise unhappy high-school career.

At least, I did until Brenda announced, on the morning of the Niagara South competition, that she was dumping both me and Andrew Horsgill to join another team with some of her snobby friends. Each team needed a minimum of three members, and we couldn't get anyone else to hook up with us under such short notice. Brenda's team won and went on to become champions at a North America–wide competition in Illinois a few months later. So Brenda Foxworthy was the 1986 problem-solving champion; she accepted a trophy at a banquet in Chicago while I sat alone in my room feeling like a loser.

Preet had the inside scoop on Brenda's house because he'd been there before. They had gone out for a month, culminating in a final date when they had sex on Brenda's bed while her parents were at a Lions Club banquet. She dumped him the next day. That was three weeks ago. Preet looked like he was going to cry when he told me. Red-faced, he confessed she'd made a disparaging remark about his penis. "She's got a gigantic stuffed animal sitting next to her bed. How was I supposed to keep my dick hard with that fucked-up thing right next to me?" Out of respect for Preet, I managed not to laugh. But I did try to picture him and her naked together. I'd never even seen another guy's cock—I had a shy bladder and preferred bathroom stalls to awkward rows of public urinals.

But Preet's erection malfunction wasn't the only reason for

the abrupt break-up. She told him that she needed a boyfriend with a more wholesome image because of her parents' standing in the community. Preet was one of the most clean-cut guys in our whole school. The only way he differed from Brenda's other boyfriends was the colour of his skin. Soon after, Brenda started dating Angelo Mancuso, a nineteen-year-old with a dumb gaze and a five o'clock shadow. I found it bizarre that she'd dumped Preet, then started seeing Angelo. Her family and friends were such WASPs, I was surprised they would even consider an Italian guy to be white. But his parents owned a construction company.

Rickie had her own reasons for hating Brenda, but she wouldn't tell either of us. I only knew because I saw what happened. It was at the end of football season, the day our team kicked Westlane High's asses. The cool kids had spiked their 7-Eleven Slurpees with gin at the game, and everyone was acting punchy. I was kinda surprised to see Rickie there. Then again, same with me, but for weeks it was all anyone talked about. It was more or less mandatory; afternoon classes had been cancelled so everyone could go to the game. I'd tried to hide in the school library, but they shut it down for the rest of the day.

In a less-populated corner of the football field, I saw Brenda beckon for Rickie to follow her behind the bleachers. This was weird; I sneaked closer to see. Brenda kissed Rickie full on the lips and took Rickie's hand and placed it on one of her breasts. After a few seconds, she pulled away. Brenda stared at Rickie. From where I stood, I couldn't see Rickie's face. "There," Brenda said. "At least now you know you're not a faggot, anyway." She walked away. I was confused. What a weird thing to say. Rick wasn't even a guy, right? It was some stupid prank. I never mentioned it to Rickie because I wouldn't know what to say.

Part of me wished I understood why Brenda liked to hurt people. The other part of me only wanted to hurt her back.

I might never have dared if not for Preet. The whole thing was his idea, and Rickie had enthusiastically agreed. I was afraid—but liked the idea of getting revenge for the first time ever. If Rickie and Preet were in, I was in. After all, it was me who supplied the knife. Grow some balls, I reminded myself. That's what my boss Ed had said to me after I said "uncle," and he finally released my face from the aroma of his armpit. He'd looked disappointed in me, staring after me as I walked away.

Turning onto Stamford Green Drive, we reached Brenda's house. Her red Camaro was nowhere to be seen—but a brown Lincoln Continental, presumably her parents', sat at the far end of the driveway. Some lights were on in the house.

Preet slowed down, pulled just past the Foxworthy residence, and parked in front of the next-door neighbours' house—far enough not to be noticed, but close enough for a quick getaway. Despite the air conditioning, I was clammy.

"Remember everything we talked about?" Preet asked quietly.

We both nodded. Preet handed me the heavy metal hook, and I put it into my knapsack.

"Any questions?"

We shook our heads.

"We have to be extremely quiet starting now. Got it?"

We nodded. Preet opened the door and got out, and we followed suit. Closing our doors as quietly as possible, we tiptoed through the far edge of the yard toward Brenda's second-storey bedroom window, on the west side of the house.

Her light had been left on. As Preet had anticipated, Brenda's window was open. And, as he had already told us, the sill was made of painted wood. I unzipped my knapsack and handed the rope and the hook to Preet. He had explained that it was an extra-strong piton used by his older brothers when they went rock climbing. It was so heavy it practically hurt my arm when I pulled it out of the sack. I guess I needed to grow some biceps too.

He secured the thick length of rope to the piton, angling it with the sharp talon facing forward. Preet launched it toward Brenda's window where it landed on the sill and sunk into it with a muted thunk. Thank God for all his years of basketball—if it had been me, I'd have broken a downstairs window or missed the house altogether. I sucked at sports. I couldn't throw or kick to save my life. Not that I'd done much of either. Who knew if I had any athletic talent or decent aim? I usually seized up with fear any time people even looked at me.

Preet turned and smiled. Rickie gave a thumbs-up. Preet walked over to where the rope hung down neatly along the side of the house and gave it three or four firm tugs. He started to climb up.

Once he reached the top and clambered inside, Preet gestured for Rickie to follow. I watched with amazement as the piton held in place, supporting her beefy frame as she scaled the side of the house. She pushed her way through the window frame. Now it was my turn. If Preet hadn't ordered me into silence earlier, this would have been the moment I'd have started to blubber and babble. I was terrified, but I grabbed the rope and began to hoist myself up. *So this is what it feels like to break and enter*, I thought. As I found my footing, I started to feel excited—and strangely honourable. I was a cat burglar stealing back my own dignity.

So far, so good. Once I got up about eight feet, I could see into the Foxworthy kitchen; the window was a few feet over. The room looked as spotless as if it had never been used. It was also empty, thank goodness. I kept moving, looking neither up nor down. Infinite moments later, I reached Brenda's window. I used both hands to pull myself in and tried to still my panting. The door to her bedroom was closed. I caught my breath and looked around.

Rickie quietly stalked the room, her eyes narrowing as she took in the luxurious surroundings. Brenda's four-poster bed was adorned with a sleek, white satin spread and decorated with five floral-design pillows. Next to the bed was a matching white dresser with a large built-in mirror. The glass had ornate etchings around the edges.

On the dresser sat the *Concise Oxford English Dictionary*. Brenda would have been the kid in kindergarten who got the sixty-four-colour box of Crayolas when the rest of us made do with the eight basic hues. I had to touch the dictionary just to determine if the spine had been cracked—to see if it had ever been opened. I walked over and picked it up and then saw something next to it that startled and surprised me. A little bound book with a chocolate-brown cover and a gold lock. In fancy lettering, the cover read "My Personal Diary." It went straight into my pants pocket.

Preet stood in front of his prey in the corner of the bedroom closest to the window. He hissed at me, "Dean, give me the knife!" I removed the compact orange knapsack from my back and tossed it to him. In it was the largest knife from the Ginsu set my dad ordered for my mom from TV last year. Preet pulled it out. The blade was large, with serrated teeth.

He stood in front of an extra-large stuffed teddy bear, which wore a yellow felt hat as big as my head. It was over three feet tall, even seated. The bear's plush fur was dark brown, with a lighter tan fur lining the inside of its ears, the pads of its feet, and a circle that surrounded its nose. A smile had been sewn into the fabric using thick black thread. Brenda told Preet she'd owned the stuffed animal since she was a little girl. When her parents first gave it to her, it was taller than her. Bits of fur were missing here and there, like the patchy bald spot on the back of my dad's head we weren't supposed to mention. Its eyes were two plastic hazel-coloured buttons. They looked strangely sad.

"Fuck you, bitch," Preet whispered. He stabbed the stuffed bear roughly below its throat, pulling the blade out and shoving it back in several times in a downward motion until he'd carved a jagged line that would have split an animal's rib cage in two. Though gutted, it still offered that same sad smile. Rickie and I watched in silence as he kicked the bear between its legs several times, causing its white Styrofoam-ball innards to fly across the room.

Rickie walked over to Brenda's dresser and took a tube of crimson lipstick from an open box full of jewellery and makeup. She applied it to the stuffed bear's lips, giving it a surreal sneer, like a circus clown. She looked at Preet and put out her hand. He handed over the knife. Rickie used it to cut the bear's head right off and dropped it on the floor in front of the ruined animal. I was startled by my friends' violence, but I felt almost as if I had had a match, I might have set the decapitated bear on fire.

That's when I noticed the trophy, a pewter cup with handles on both sides fixed to a wooden base. It sat on a small white table between the bedroom and closet doors, next to a miniature clock encased in a glass dome. A small metal plate was screwed onto the base of the trophy, upon which the words "Tomorrow's Leaders Problem-Solving Contest, Chicago Illinois, First Place" were engraved. I stared at it blankly, unable to draw my eyes away.

Preet looked at me, then at the trophy. He walked to the dresser, grabbed the winner's cup, and placed it on the floor in front of him. Unzipping his pants, he reached into his underwear, pulled out his penis, and began to urinate into the trophy in a steaming waterfall.

"Whoah, man!" Rickie called out in shock. No matter what Brenda had said, Preet's dick looked beautiful to me. I couldn't help but stare. Rickie was gazing right at Preet's pecker too, as gushes of urine pumped out of it and poured into that goddamned trophy cup. As Preet's stream slowed to a trickle, I wondered if I could get over my pee-shyness and fill it up the rest of the way myself.

Right then the bedroom door pushed open. Brenda's little sister Becki, her head barely reaching the doorknob, stepped into the room, pointed at Preet's penis, and screamed. Preet stuffed it back in his pants and darted toward the window, Rickie lumbering directly behind him. Becki continued to shriek all the while. I heard a rumble from behind her as someone started up the stairs.

I looked over at the overflowing trophy cup. I took two steps toward it, then stopped. I felt a moment of inner calm. With the inside of my right foot, I kicked the trophy's base as hard as I could. With immaculate aim, the trophy, as well as a torrent of piss, arced into the air toward the corner of the room, the trophy landing upside down on top of the bear, right where its head used to be, before ending upright at its feet.

A wave of euphoria I'd never experienced before passed through me. I felt like the star football player who'd just kicked a fifty-yard field goal and won the game. Becki continued to scream. I took one more look at the yellow-stained bear and the trophy at its feet, the rim of its cup still wet with drops of Preet's urine. I grabbed the knife and threw it in the knapsack. Bolting for the window, I tossed the sack out and started to climb down the rope.

Halfway to the bottom, I heard the squeal of tires as Preet and Rickie pulled away. I heard Mr Foxworthy in the front yard call out after them. I inched down the rope as quietly as I could, making it down the side of the house without being detected.

When I reached the ground, I grabbed the knapsack and hopped the fence onto their next-door neighbour's property, traversed the yard to the far side, and emerged onto the sidewalk.

I could hear Mr and Mrs Foxworthy talking on the porch. I walked past their front yard slowly, like any local boy on my way to the neighbourhood Dairy Queen. If there was one thing I knew for sure, I didn't grow up in that neighbourhood, and the Foxworthys wouldn't know me from Adam. Without stopping, I passed their house and headed up the street.

I turned off Stamford Green and onto Portage Road and headed for home, nearly an hour's walk. I could walk all night without getting tired; I felt cool despite the heat. I approached the Five Corners and stood across from the bank waiting for the light to change. A familiar-looking white sports car pulled up to the corner and stopped at the amber light. The driver tossed an empty cigarette pack out the window. It hit my foot. Craven A Menthols.

I didn't look up. Instead, I walked over to the black metal bin next to the bank machine, pulled out Brenda Foxworthy's stolen diary, and dropped it into the trash. The traffic light changed, and I crossed the street.

TAKING CREATIVE LICENSE

for Mark Andrew Hamilton

JENNA IS TWEETING when she's supposed to be painting. *Ennui is the religion of my generation.* The singer from her favourite band updates his own Twitter feed as she refreshes her browser. She's in a small white room that smells like oil paints. Apparently, he sits in a Calgary university library with aching lumbar muscles.

Man. Since when did my lower back decide to turn 65 while the rest of me remains 30? Get me a stretcher

Jenna is alone in her studio, unprotected from the summer heat outside. Over the speaker, his pretty male voice coos over a single strummed acoustic guitar and sweet piano triads. She cranks the volume and stands, waltzing with an imaginary partner.

The object of her obsession is gay. And in her own reverie, slender, blonde Jenna is more to his liking. She's a muscular older man with a thick black beard and calm dark eyes. Her flimsy yellow baby T is instead a plaid flannel work shirt, filled out by testosterone and marked with sweat. Her second-hand cargo pants from Value Village are instead some kind of uniform—a janitor, a streetcar driver, a night watchman. Her thin wrists and forearms are thick and strong, corrugated with a dense patchwork of salt-and-pepper curls. Her voice is deep as a cave, and the natural opiate of her masculine embrace could soothe an emotional young man, ease gentle sobs to quiet.

She walks the perimeter of her white-painted artist's studio, from the window views a Bavarian forest instead of a Parkdale pharmacy, listens to cicadas rather than car honks and the non-sequitur bellows of a street fight below. *My darling Luke would love me like this*, she thinks. *Together in the woods, I'd be his father figure, and he'd be my submissive soul mate.* She would lie down on top of him, oppressing his limbs with her burly weight and height, as he squirmed and giggled on a blanket of pine needles, smiling. In a single movement, she would flip him over onto his belly. She'd fix his sore back for him. Or at least take his mind off it.

Fingertips to MacBook again, Jenna concocts a new, fake Twitter identity with a picture of a good-looking trucker she finds on Google Images. She calls herself @PaulBunyan. @Paul posts a flirty reply directed at the Alberta troubadour Jenna's crushing on. *I happen to be very good at lower-back massages, young man.* Even on Twitter, she puts periods at the end of her sentences. Self-assured. Definitive.

Jenna lies down on the clean wooden floor of her studio, the nearby canvas almost untouched since her arrival three hours ago. Her ex, Gabe, will be here any minute now. They are going to a show together, to see two bands she hates. The Mountain Goats are too nerdy and the New Pornographers too raucous. She likes delicate music. Gabe always tells her she's such a gaylord.

Gabe is crude and noisy himself, but he doesn't judge her for being so weird, and he won't ask why she hasn't finished the last painting, even though her show is in two days. Instead, he will hork at random as they manoeuvre the busy downtown sidewalks and dart between buildings to take a piss whenever he feels like it, barely out of view. Gabe sometimes picks his nose and eats it right in front of her. Jenna feels a lot of affection for this boy, but she's glad they aren't kissing or messing around anymore.

They go to concerts together because Gabe's new girl, Mindie, doesn't like bands. She's only into her religion, which believes that dead people are just sleeping. At the second coming, they wake up. On the plus side for Gabe, her religion also doesn't believe in using condoms. "I'm gettin' it wet," he will say just to get on Jenna's nerves.

She closes her eyes and thinks again of the handsome singer serenading her as the song switches in iTunes. He's wearing a yellow parka and a tartan sweater, and his tender blue-eyed gaze is fixed on hers. He romps toward Jenna through the snow-covered trees, red-bearded and smiling. Jenna slides her finger down her pants. They kiss.

The concert was tedious. Moody songs about the Bible. Jenna liked it better when the Mountain Goats sang about crystal meth and robbery. Up the street from the show, she and Gabe sit under fluorescents. All day breakfast all night long. He stabs the yolk with his fork and then mashes it like a bright yellow zit.

"I'm surprised Mindie didn't want to hear that. Isn't she into Deuteronomy?" Jenna cuts her bacon strip into seven one-inch squares and passes the first one between her lips.

"She doesn't like to be around people who drink alcohol," he replies flatly. Gabe grabs his half-litre of Neilson's chocolate milk and tips it into his mouth for a few open-mouthed chugs. Neither Gabe nor Jenna drink booze either.

He belches, but it isn't a loud one. Jenna has one hand on the ketchup bottle even though she doesn't like it. Gabe grabs the bottle from the top and tugs it out of her hand. He smothers his home fries.

Jenna lightly butters her French toast. The old blackened knife looks like it's been used to heat hashish. *Stoners in the kitchen*, she thinks, glancing back to see an elderly man with a round belly in a thin grey apron and sweat-steeped tam. *Hmm.* Gabe used to make her French toast when they were dating. He knew she didn't like syrup so he made it her way, savoury, and tossed oregano and pepper flakes into the eggy mixture.

Gabe would cook in his underwear. More rugged than

handsome, he had a naturally athletic body with arms he didn't even have to work for. Luck of the Portuguese. When he returned to her kitchen with the stack of plates, you could see a tuft of hair poking out just above his butt in the white Unicos. One day, taking creative license, she excised them with a Lady Bic razor when he was asleep on his belly, and he didn't even wake up. She mixed the hairs into one of her paints. It was her first painting that sold to someone she didn't know.

"Do you need to get back to her before you turn into a pumpkin? Or a Satanic imp?" Gabe has dated the new girl for almost a year, and he's allowed out on Fridays. Mindie watches *Everybody Loves Raymond* reruns and then goes to bed. Gabe alternates between street hockey with the guys and music with Jenna.

Gabe picks his nose behind his napkin. He sticks it on the serviette and folds it over, then wipes his mouth on the booger-free part.

"She just told me she's pregnant." Gabe pulls his BlackBerry out of his pants pocket, looks at the time, and stuffs it back in. He doesn't wear a watch.

Jenna eyes the waitress's approach down the long corridor of the restaurant as she puts the last perfectly cubed piece of toast in her mouth. She's been working here longer than Jenna has lived in the city. Jenna likes her very pink nail polish. She looks back at Gabe.

"What are you going to do?"

"It's not up to me, is it?" He pushes his plate away. Gabe stands up, pulls a twenty out, and puts it on the table. "Gotta take a leak." He hitches up his pants and heads downstairs for the can.

"Your plate is spotless," the waitress says. She puts Gabe's, a sea of red and yellow liquid splotches, on top of Jenna's naked one, efficiently stacking the two of them with cutlery and all the disposables from the tabletop. Walks away, the back of her blue skirt accented with a lopsided white bow.

Back in the studio by herself, with one hand braced on the desk, Jenna fucks herself with a UHU glue stick. Her forehead drips with sweat. She smells the grease from the restaurant on the jean jacket at her feet. Her black pants and olive cotton panties are pulled down around her ankles. The rectangle of the laptop screen glows, a pulsing LED shoebox in the otherwise dark room. The window is open. Outside, junkies yell at each other about something again.

judging from your tiny twitter photo, i'd most definitely let you give me that massage, @PaulBunyan

One minute, she's a bearded high-school coach, making that Calgarian singer do 100 pushups in a pair of tattered grey sweatpants, stepping on his back with the worn sneaker of authority, so he's unable to rise. The next, she's a nerd from a high-school glee club, and she and Luke are teenaged boys, stroking one another's faces, clad in pyjamas, with twin erections tented toward one another. Then she's back in the art studio. Luke is playing with her vagina like it's the first one he's seen, stroking himself and poised to enter her. And Gabe's sweaty foreskin slaps her cheek, so she opens her mouth. Then it's just the two of them again, Jenna laying on her back with Luke's bearded chin connected to her wet pussy, his nose bumping her clitoris and sliding around it as she bucks, looking up at her own paintings, which for once seem less abstract than usual.

Jenna punches her own clit five times with the ball of her hand, and she's done. The glue stick falls out of her other hand to the floor.

She closes one of the tabs on her web browser, a video of Luke and bandmates busking in a park in London, England. As the tune had hit its emotional crescendo, she got off. It did feel odd that some young kids were watching the band in the video as she frigged herself. She goes back to the Twitter page and taps out a reply from @PaulBunyan.

It would be hard to keep my hands on your back muscles. I know they would want to roam lower.

Funny she had incorporated Gabe into the sex fantasy. He would never get into a scene with two guys. The time they brought home a girl from a club had been a disaster.

By three a.m., Jenna feels wiped. The apartment is three blocks away, but she needs to get painting again first thing in the morning. She pulls the sleeping bag out of the corner, unfolds it under the studio window, and lays on top. A cool breeze blows over her. She likes her own sweet smell on her hands.

Jenna hears her phone vibrate in the middle of her crumpled pile of pants over by the desk. She closes her eyes.

Jenna is painting, but the canvas she couldn't fill yesterday remains untouched. Sitting in the chair, she has a Filbert brush in one hand and a white Riddell football helmet in the other, purchased off eBay. She's turned the left side a solid black. On the right, she creates a green dinosaur wearing a yellow crown about to eat a red car. She stole the idea from a Montreal painter she admires but doesn't think he'll mind the tribute, if he even hears of it. If anything, she feels strange putting nine hand-painted football helmets in the show simply because she knows they will sell if nothing else does. *But a girl's gotta eat*, she tells herself.

When the helmet feels complete, she puts it down on the worktable. Her phone vibrates over on the desk. *Just when I need a distraction, it comes at the perfect moment.* Magical thinking.

"What's up? I called you last night."

"I just finished something. I need a break." The sun is starting to heat the studio. Jenna wants to go home to shower and change.

"Free for lunch?"

Gabe never hangs with her on a Saturday. "Yeah, sure, bro."

"Oh yeah," he said. "I was on the Soundscapes website this morning. That Calgary band you like is in town next month. Want to go?"

"Cool. I'd love it," she says.

"I'll pick up tickets."

"I'll give you money."

"Cool."

"Let's meet at the red brick place, College and Palmerston. The patio must be open. Give me an hour. I need to shower." She hangs up, puts down the phone, and logs on. Seven guys have added @PaulBunyan on Twitter overnight. She has a DM from Luke.

thanks for the offer handsome. i've got a bf though

Jenna smiles. She reciprocates the adds from the other guys. Gets up and puts on her shoes.

The meal is all small talk till Gabe pushes his finished plate away.

"The baby isn't mine." He says it like he's commenting on the weather. "She's been getting it from the youth pastor at the Seventh-day Adventist church. She's moving to Brampton to shack up with him."

Jenna touches Gabe's hand. "She belongs in Brampton."

"I feel dead." He looks like he's going to cry and actually wipes at his eyes with his messy napkin.

"Resurrect yourself. Somebody's got to help me set up at New Gallery tomorrow. I need a bartender too. It's a good thing you've got time on your hands all of a sudden. I've really got to get back to the studio. Walk me."

Gabe looks down at his remaining swirls of gravy.

Jenna pushes her chair back. "I've got to pee. Back in a minute." She rubs his neck for a second as she passes by.

On the toilet, Jenna takes out her phone and tweets a reply to Luke's direct message while urinating. *No worries, friend. I don't think it would work between us anyway. See you in T.O. I'll be the bearded guy at the back of the club. Smiling.* Her character count down to zero, Jenna wipes herself after putting the iPhone down. *Enough of that.* She's supposed to be painting.

MAN, WOMAN, AND CHILD

KATE LIKED TO FLIRT WITH THE LETTER CARRIER even though she suspected he was gay. She appreciated a challenge, craved variety. His portly build and short stature reminded her of Al Waxman from *King of Kensington*, only the new mailman was terminally shy. His trim beard and baby face conjured Maher Arar's chubby younger brother. She knew it was silly, but she liked the way he knocked on the door. Slow and sturdy. He was the opposite of her husband Sean, a tall, hyperactive wall of muscle.

It was all glances and smiles, cocking her head at an almost imperceptible angle through the half-opened door. The man in blue was already blushing, and they hadn't exchanged a word. He stood before her with a brown cardboard box the size of a kindergarten boy on an industrial-grade metal dolly.

"This parcel is for Les Montague." The letter carrier read from a yellow piece of paper affixed to the metal clipboard in his hand. He was sweating—from his exertion and the summer heat rather than Kate's magnetic lure, she surmised. "Our downstairs neighbour." Les was Kate and Sean's tenant. Sean thought him bizarre, but Kate knew Les was just misunderstood. He rarely left his room. Like Kate, he worked from home. She was an accountant; she didn't know exactly what Les did. "I think he's home right now. If not, can I sign for it?"

He looked down at his clipboard to verify the status of a particular checkbox. "I can actually leave it on the porch. No signature required." He looked up and made eye contact with Kate for the first time. Brown eyes. "It's pretty heavy." He handed her a few small envelopes from his sack.

"Do you think you could bring it inside? I have no idea what's in there, and it's supposed to get pretty muggy today." The only time Kate had been successful with her mailman machinations, the letter carrier was a woman. Her name was Verlia, and last summer they had a three-month affair.

He put down his mailbag and tilted back the dolly. "Can you hold the door, ma'am?" Behind him, on the sidewalk, a little boy in green shorts straddled a tricycle and sped across the sidewalk past the mail truck. Kate stepped forward and held the screen door open. The letter carrier brushed against her as he pushed the dolly into her foyer. She liked his smell.

"Take it right to the door halfway down the hall, past the living room." She followed him inside, dropping the letters on the hall bureau as she passed. They stood together at the top of the stairs. Kate put her hand on his shoulder.

"I know this is asking a lot, but would you mind taking it down the stairs and leaving it in front of that door?" There were only a dozen steps, but he did say it was heavy. Without a word, he leaned back and rolled the dolly slowly downward, bending at his knees. She could see the package was weighty from the way it rocked a bit on each step. The letter carrier had a patch of sweat on his lower back. Kate gazed at it as if it were a Rorschach ink-blot, but couldn't decide what it resembled. At the bottom of the stairs, he yanked the dolly out and pulled it back up. He stopped at the top.

"What's your name?" she asked.

"Rish, ma'am."

"Thanks a ton, Rish. I'm Kate."

Below them, the box sat at the entrance to Les's basement apartment.

The intermittent thunks from downstairs were annoying the piss out of Sean. Les must've been to IKEA. Sean decided to check the garbage later for boxes. There was no point in asking the weirdo, who kept to himself to the point of seclusion. Sean couldn't picture Les shopping; he'd rarely even seen him leave the basement. They had inherited Les two years ago when Kate's dad moved to New Zealand to be a gay man and gave them the house.

"He won't cause you any trouble," Kate's dad had said when he made the offer. Sean doubted his words; the gift house felt like a subtle indictment of Sean's own inability to provide for Kate, his failure to sire a grandchild. Now he hoped that Les, the basement gnome, wasn't engaged in some kind of major construction.

Sean stripped down in the upstairs bathroom and turned on the hot and cold taps. He pulled the shower curtain across and soaped himself up, paying attention to his thick blond hair and his rank underarms and dirty ass. Fencing practice made him sweat and stink, but he preferred to shower at home, even though the claw-foot tub was small and he always got water on the floor. Sean was built tall and wide like a refrigerator. He had to negotiate his own bathroom like a gorilla trying to get into the driver's seat of a Cooper Mini. But something about the shower room at the Salle D'Armes unnerved him too. The men's changing facilities were so spare, the tiled floors so cold and ancient and cracked. Each showerhead was a mere nozzle jutting from a section of metal piping. A dozen guys scrubbed down, a few feet apart, fully exposed. The water was always too hot. And the room made Sean think of a gas chamber.

The woman at the front desk knew not to give him a towel when he came. He thought he noticed her staring on a few occasions.

"She wants your piggy in her blanket," said his brother Daniel, who was also Sean's fencing buddy. Danny sometimes talked bitchy like one of those drag queens, like RuPaul, only he was short, freckled, skinny, and white. Daniel and Sean looked nothing alike.

"Bro, didn't she see my ring?" Sean thought chicks who went after married men were scummy. He wasn't interested.

He poured a capful of Head & Shoulders into his hands and massaged his scalp. The banging started up again. It persisted for a minute, stopped, then picked back up again. *Jackass.* Sean felt the urge to go downstairs and build the Bennø CD rack or Bërgsbo bookcase for Les himself. And instruct him to load it up quietly. Sean suspected Les was intimidated by his build and demeanour—or at least he hoped so—but clearly not enough to fear his wrath for making such a racket. *This guy's got no respect,* thought Sean.

"Goddamn, what the fuck," Sean muttered as he rinsed his hair then turned off the water. He grabbed a towel and pawed at himself with it. Pulling on a pair of gym shorts and a tank top, he stepped on a pile of Kate's bras and panties on the floor as he hurried out of the bathroom and down the stairs. The phone rang, but he ignored it as he reached Les's door and rapped three times.

I've got my adult Nuk from Pacifiers R Us in my mouth, but I'd so much rather be suckling a woman's breast. Especially if she's lactating.

My former therapist, Dr Zirknitz, says I like to dress like a baby because I abandoned my girlfriend and newborn son when I was eighteen. I think that's simplistic and predictable. I believe you can like something for no reason, or at least no significant reason. Milly and the boy still live in Hull. I send cheques every month.

I've got my favourite XL onesie on. It's black with yellow rings around the collar and arm- and leg-holes. It has a picture of a giraffe on it. I bought it on eBay for twenty-five dollars. I picked it because it reminds me of the home uniform of the Pittsburgh Penguins. Also, I like dark colours, nothing too flashy.

There are forty-six baby outfits in my closet. You can afford to indulge a little bit when you're a highly paid human-rights consultant. I help people challenge mistreatment at the hands of the municipal, provincial, and federal governments. Right now I'm working on the case of a refugee who's a part-time postal worker. She was sexually harassed—a pair of managers ganged up on her in the postal-sortation plant at the end of the night shift. I hate this kind of unspeakable bullshit, and I am very good at avenging it. We are going to win this case.

I'm finally moving out of this dungeon in a month. I just gave Kate my notice this morning. But some things can't wait. My adult-sized crib was delivered this morning. I didn't see it till after dinner time because I was meeting the lawyers in Avizeh's case. It took me two hours to put the gorgeous contraption together, including an interruption from that meathead Sean. But I followed the instructions, and it holds my weight. I'm lying in it right now. I've got two rooms down here, in addition to my own bathroom. The living room looks like any seventies rec room, but the bedroom is my baby haven. I've managed to keep that obnoxious goon from stepping too far onto my turf. Kate's father used to leave me alone. He was a very polite man.

I used to think I took a basement apartment because of shame or guilt about my adult-baby lifestyle. I started to see Zirknitz in an effort to sort through those feelings. What a waste of time. The old fool thinks everything in my life—my relationship to my mother, my choice of employment, my thoughts on my own penis size—ties into my life as an AB. I think it's all bullshit. I'm moving into an expensive condo; I can afford it. So what if the movers balk at moving a crib that holds a man who's thirty-one, five-nine, and weighs 205? I don't need to hide. I do, however, need my diaper changed.

A trio of firm knocks on the door. Perfect timing.

Kate had missed her period for the first time in a long, long time. Nineteen days late. She was usually like clockwork.

"How was the flight, Dad?" Auckland to Sydney. For a funeral.

"Long, Kat. The movie made me cry. I'm not up for this." Over Skype from his hotel room, Kate's father's voice had a computerized texture reminiscent of the chorus of Styx's "Mr. Roboto." He had dated a man from Sydney named David for a year, but it didn't work out. David had been a very large man. One day, he just didn't wake up. This would be the first time her father had seen him since the breakup. She didn't know whether to pray for a closed casket or an open one. *At the very least, a sturdy one*, she thought.

"I'm sorry." Kate was organizing a pile of financial ledgers while she talked. As she put the top half of the stack down, the phone cord strummed against her left nipple. It felt sore.

"I could use some good news for a change, that's for sure."

She took this as her prompt. "I think I'm pregnant."

Excited, his voice sped up, rattling off questions without waiting for a reply. "Are you sure? How do you feel? Do you want to keep it? I didn't think Sean had it in him. Always figured that dick was shooting blanks."

"I'm not sure." Kate fanned herself with a balance sheet. The central air was on the fritz again. She had asked Sean to take a look, but she would just have to call the repair guys herself later today.

Her father's voice cracked. "I love you, Katty. Whatever you want to do, I support you. I love you so much." *The impending funeral*, she thought. *That's why he's over-emotional.* She decided to pick up a pregnancy test. And make a doctor's appointment.

"Feel better, Dad. Call me again after the service, okay?"

Kate traced in her mind the times she'd messed around recently. Sean's brother Danny had put it in for a few strokes before she'd got a condom on him. Kate put the phone down and placed her client's financial papers back on the desk. She needed to get outside. A walk to the bank. Get the rent cheque and deposit it. She walked downstairs and knocked three times on Les Montague's door.

Sean's last client was a plump lady named Mitsuyo who worked for the government. She came to Modern Fitness on her flex hours, and Sean put Mitsuyo through her paces. The elliptical machine, an increasing number of push-ups. She would never be a supermodel, but he watched as a seed of new confidence germinated within her. That's what made Sean feel good.

He wore his gym shorts and tank home. *Christ, it's humid.* The front door was cracked open when he got there. *Got to deal with that busted central air,* Sean thought. He wondered if Kate could take a break. For the first time in ages, he felt horny. Maybe it was the heat. He was developing a visible, potent chub.

Sean picked up the handful of letters on the hallway table. Three for them and two for Les. He went downstairs to slide them under the door, but found it ajar. Sean poked his head inside, and was startled to hear the sound of a crying infant. "What the ... "

The noise came from the corner bedroom. Not bothering to knock, Sean shoved the door open and strode through the basement, ducking his head for the low ceiling. Something was wrong. *If Les is hurting a kid, I'll strangle him.* Sean's rod stopped throbbing and his balls moved protectively upward. He knew something was sick about that guy. He pushed the bedroom door wide open.

The room smelled vaguely of fresh piss. Pastel blue walls festooned with a cartoon border—a recurring image of SpongeBob SquarePants chased by an electric eel wearing a lime-coloured baseball cap. The balding freak knelt inside a gargantuan wooden bedstead, balancing himself on the frame atop the vertical slats, wearing an enormous black terrycloth jumper. Kate stood shirtless next to the Brobdingnagian crib with one breast cupped in her hand. Les Montague slowly lapped at her tender aureole with a long flat tongue. He paused mid-lick, and offered Sean an infantile simper.

Sean's remnant semi-erection turned to sand in his shorts. Kate stood still, swivelling her neck to face him.

"I'm having a baby," she said. "I don't think it's yours."

THE
EDEN CLIMBER

RUTHANN WAS ALWAYS A SIMPLETON. It was true when we were children, and as true seven decades later. Glancing from my own bed to hers, I felt a tart mingling of pity and disappointment, like a sour taste at the back of my throat. But her drab cot was empty; the trio of welded steel bars that form her industrial bed rail imprisoned no one. She was in a different sort of jail: the chapel at the end of the hall. For a few hours, she traded physical incarceration for a spiritual one. I'd have smiled at my cleverness were the whole thing not so depressing.

For decades, we saw one another just once every few years at holidays, then at our parents' funerals. Little did I expect that my sister and I would share a bedroom once again, especially in as decrepit and demeaning a place as the Brentwood Pines Home for the Aged.

"Where's Ruthie, Cassandra?"

I jumped in my chair. Gildette, a large, buxom orderly, had appeared in our room. And trailing behind her, a faint, sickly sweet whiff of feces. She'd just visited Ethel Grennier next door. That ancient Quebecois biddy was a veritable shit factory, moaning and yelling about her pained bowels in nasal, sharply accented English. The pale green walls were far too thin.

"Praying," I said, picking up one of the books next to my chair—Doris Lessing's *Briefing for a Descent into Hell*—and acting as if I were reading it, to avoid further conversation.

She smiled and put something down on the tray table next to Ruthann's bed. Based on her facial features, I identified Gildette as West African, but hadn't figured out exactly where. I didn't recognize her accent. Of course, my travels in Africa were long ago.

"I brought her a photocopy of today's crossword puzzle."

"As long as it's just the *Vancouver Sun*—she's not lucid enough for the *Globe*." It was true. Five years my senior at seventy-six, Ruthann was not the sharpest hoe in the proverbial shed. Thank Christ for her magnifying bar. The last thing I wanted was to read scriptures to her or help with an infernal grade-six-level puzzle. I felt a pang of longing for the days when Rupert and I used to work on the Sunday *Times* cryptic together. That would have been far beyond Ruthann's capabilities, even back in her prime.

Gildette turned and walked away, humming. How annoying.

I peered out the window. Beyond the Brentwood Town Centre

mall, one of the North Shore mountains poked into the sky. It reminded me of Mount Fuji, which Rupert and I saw on our honeymoon. This snow-capped peak felt just as distant.

I'd just put the paperback down when I heard the telltale squeak of my sister's wheelchair and her high-pitched, animated voice accompanied by a deeper, more melodious male counterpart. I grabbed the book, opened it to a random page, and pretended to study it.

The blond, fresh-faced man who pushed Ruthann's chair was Devon, her favourite orderly. He leaned into her and nodded, staring with attentive blue eyes. His short, trim haircut gave the outward appearance of an old-fashioned, conservative male, but I wasn't fooled. The body language and physical build told a different story: he had the shallow and confident comportment of a soap-opera actor. His blue scrubs were too tight.

I am suspicious of handsome people. They never have to work as hard as the rest of us, which blemishes their character. The orderly's good looks had a single flaw: a wandering right eye that trailed behind his left for a second or two when he turned to look at you. I narrowed my gaze when he looked over, one eye lazily tracking the other.

"...and what sweet children they were," Ruthann blathered. As usual, she was deliriously happy about something. "And such beautiful voices as well."

Devon nodded and murmured something in his low, seductive register. What a gigolo. I turned a page in my book but watched them discreetly. As they continued to chatter, Devon lowered the bed rail, elevated the upper half of the adjustable bed using the control button, then carefully lifted Ruthann from the chair to the bed. I'd only seen Gildette assist her that way. I didn't know male orderlies were allowed to have such contact with the women residents. He set the tray table in front of her, grabbed a pencil out of his uniform's breast pocket, and placed it delicately next to the sheet of paper.

"Have a good afternoon, Ruthie. Maybe we should bring your sister to church next time. It might lift her spirits."

I snorted and turned another page in my paperback. Mentioning my atheism would probably only confuse him anyway. This boy was no doubt raised on apple pie and Jesus of Nazareth. Ruthann touched Devon's arm and smiled. I grimaced. I peered over my book toward the weathered yellow floor tiles and watched the orderly's blue suede running shoes recede from view. Once he was gone, I addressed my sister. "You were a lot longer than usual at chapel today, Ruthann. Why is that?"

Ruthann looked up from her crossword puzzle and smiled. "Well, first of all, we had special visitors. The Kelowna Songsters. They were very talented boys and girls."

"They came all the way from Kelowna to Burnaby to sing at the chapel of Brentwood Pines?"

Ruthann nodded excitedly. "They sang a song by Janet Jackson!"

I've never been impressed by my sister's devotion to the church, but I'm always amused by religious hypocrisy. I could imagine few celebrities more godless than the Jacksons. I tutted with mock indignation, pleased with myself. "That doesn't sound very Christian to me."

"It was uplifting," Ruthann protested with a benign smile. "After that, Devon and I practiced for tomorrow's wheelchair race."

I gave her a withering look. A few days ago, an announcement was made in the lunch room about a wheelchair race to be held in the auditorium downstairs. I hadn't been down those stairs since I got here three months ago. Loath as I was to make the effort tomorrow, I wanted to keep a watchful eye on that suspect orderly.

"Why are you doing that with Devon? Why don't you race with Rory's help instead?" Rory was the other male intern on our floor. A long-haired, fat homosexual, he was fond of quoting Bette Davis while pushing Ruthann around in her wheelchair. If I ever reach the point where I'm reliant upon someone like that for my own mobility, I will end my life. This cane is torture enough. On further thought, maybe a chair might be better. My bunions make it feel like I'm walking with stones underfoot, and these ugly old-person shoes they gave me aren't helping.

"Devon is a lot stronger than Rory, I'm sure of that!" Ruthann giggled.

"Nonsense. Rory is twice his size. You'd have a much better chance of winning."

"The person on your support team is only allowed to help you turn the corners around the pylons," Ruthann corrected me. "The race will be a test of my own efforts."

I sighed, and she continued.

"The Songsters will be there to sing a song and cheer us on. Then they are off to a benefit concert for VANDU, a support group for drug addicts in Vancouver."

How preposterous. Wasn't Vandu the name of the killer whale at Marineland? Ruthann needed to get her hearing checked. I made a note to interrupt Gildette's infernal humming the very next day to have that arranged.

"Well, make sure Devon keeps his hands on the handlebars and off your shoulders. I don't trust him."

Ruthann went blank and looked down at her crossword. Scanning the clues, a look of confusion crossed her face.

I emitted gas. Grasping my cane with my right hand, I stood slowly and began to make my way to the toilet. I needed a bit of alone time. With any luck, Ruthann would fall asleep while I was in there, and I'll have some peace and quiet between now and dinner time.

Dinner. Speckled mush that resembled puréed carrots but tasted like wheat paste. I missed real food.

"Well, Liza from the dementia ward has been with him, and she says that he's got one fine instrument—and he knows how to play it too!"

I sat at the smallest table in the grey dining hall, which I had all to myself. It was right by the open kitchen and also near the exit. This allowed me to get in and out of there as quickly as possible. My ears pricked up when I heard these bits of conversation from the nearby kitchen, accompanied by tawdry laughter. I figured out quickly who they were talking about.

"Better a skin flute than a skin piccolo, I guess!" I recognized the voice of Rory, the gay orderly. It was deeper than the others, but still possessed feminine characteristics.

Another woman replied. "The way she said it, it sounded like the *tuba* of love!"

Laughter erupted in the open kitchen. At the table nearest me, a bald man with thick plastic eyeglasses dumped a forkful of greens into his juice. Low murmurs filled the dining room, punctuated occasionally by one large woman's even larger voice. The one with Tourette's—what was her name?

"Suck my knob!" she bellowed. Her outburst hung in the air. With her right arm, she deliberately knocked over someone's glass, spilling liquid all over the table. A man across from her wearing a fuzzy wool vest began to cry, shoulders convulsing. I had to look away.

Through the kitchen doorway, I could see the bustle of orderlies assembling the last of the evening's meal for the people they had to feed themselves. I fingered the fork on my tray, unable to take another bite of the dreadful meal. Another orderly spoke.

"Rory, you've probably seen it in the little boys' room. How does Devon measure up?"

"Standing at the urinals, the last thing I do is stare at other guys' packages. That's a great way to lose a tooth or two." The tubby, effete one's voice affected mock indignation. He paused before adding, "It's a nice size—but I've seen bigger!"

Gildette laughed the loudest. How could she be entertained by these low-class, distasteful musings? Surely her culture must disapprove of male homosexuality. Nigeria, could it be?

Five orderlies emerged from the kitchen at once, fanning out into the room of hungry invalids like geese in formation. Rory aimed straight for me. In the fluorescent lights of the cafeteria, I noticed that his brown and grey roots were starting to show in the midst of his unnatural yellow coiffure.

"How are you doing today, Cassie?" His voice reminded me of a young girl addressing a kindergarten teacher and trying to gain her favour, polished apple in hand.

"Don't call me Cassie. My name is Cassandra."

He placed a hand on his hip and arched his eyebrows. "Well, forgive me, Ca-*son*-dra. Would you be so kind as to tell me where I could find your sister, Ruthie? And pray tell, why isn't she with you?"

Such priggery. I wished I could make this turd simply vanish. I closed my eyes for a second, then opened them. He was still there, a weighty tray quivering in his hand.

"She fell asleep from exhaustion. The *Sun* crossword proved too much for her."

"Hmm. Then I'll have to bring this to her in your room and feed her there." With that, he turned on his heel and sauntered off in a rather ladylike fashion.

I didn't bother to stifle my belch. Wonderful. I can't even return to my own room—such as it is—without more nuisance from the haughty invert. Rupert befriended a few homosexuals when he taught at the university, but the older I get, the less I can tolerate their ways. Ruthann, for all her supposed piety, doesn't mind them. Of course, there is no internal logic to her scattered belief system. She thinks it's a good thing that a youth choir is going to sing for a bunch of heroin addicts!

I took my cane from the empty chair beside me and stood up. It felt heavy. It hurt to stand, and not from my bunions. No, sometimes the weight you feel when trying to raise yourself is purely emotional. Trying to guard my feeble sister, while maintaining my own dignity—it can be too much to bear.

Walking slowly down the hall, I came into the rotunda and made my way toward the window. The sun was beginning to set, giving the sky a rosy, sombre hue. From the window I could see the rose garden below, and still make out the peach- and lemon-coloured blossoms. The bushes needed pruning, though I doubted that would happen.

The last time I'd looked at the roses was the first week I was here. Rupert had been dead for three months, and Ruthann's daughter in Ottawa began to pressure me to come and stay with her mother. What else did I have going on back in Calgary, my niece pointed out. It was true; I'd not been much of a faculty wife and had never gotten along well with the others. Rupert and I didn't socialize much anyway; we had each other, and that was all we needed. After a couple of courtesy calls in the first few weeks, I was truly alone.

Because Ruthann was sensitive to pollen, I had gone out to the garden on my own. Despite the void I felt, I had to admit the roses were delicate and beautiful. Away from the grove of colourful bushes, along a lattice fence, the Eden Climber grew, with its full and heavy complement of dense petals, white on the outer edges and the colour of pink grapefruit on the inside.

I sat in the shade on a concrete patio off to the side, with no one else nearby. I looked down at the white slabs and noticed some large black ants. Three or four wandered their own paths, with no apparent rhyme or reason.

One approached me. It moved more quickly than the other ants, carrying something. Staring with curiosity, I noticed that it had the body of another ant, lengthwise, in its mouth. It ran frantically to my left, then turned and dashed off to my right. After a while of going nowhere fast, it placed the body of the other ant on the ground, touched it two times with its head, and ran off. It scurried away from the rose bushes and grass, farther onto the concrete toward the red brick wall of Brentwood Pines. I continued to stare until the departing ant was gone from view altogether.

The clock on my bedside table read ten-thirty. Our captors don't usually let us sleep this late—they must have forgotten about me. Ruthann's bed was empty. I remembered the wheel-chair race.

I dragged myself toward our bathroom, rubbing my eyes, trying to emerge from the foggy haze of sleep. As I sat on the toilet, I recalled a conversation with Ruthann earlier in the week. She was looking forward to her daughter Joelle's visit later this month, and she mentioned Emily Bertolini, who lived on the first floor. At ninety-one, she still had visitors weekly, including cousins who travelled here from Italy.

My sister somehow knew and was able to recall a lot of personal information about many people at Brentwood Pines. Ruthann had shrugged when I mentioned this. "God is in the details," she replied, as some kind of mystical rejoinder. I doubt she even knew who originally said that. She'd probably heard it regurgitated at that multi-denominational, Janet Jackson–condoning chapel of quackery up the hall. I realized I didn't know anyone else's name in this place—except for Ruthann and the orderlies we saw every day.

As I sat back on my bed with my terry bathrobe on, Gildette entered the room with a tray, which she brought to my bedside.

In a mock-indignant tone, she called out loudly. "Cassandra, I've had to bring your breakfast in here three days in a row. You need to have breakfast with the others, every day!"

Her voice hurt my ears. I looked down as she lifted the lid on the tray to reveal a steaming omelette accompanied by pear slices out of a can. I poked at the omelette with a fork. It appeared to have last night's spinach folded inside.

"Thank you, Gildette." I was more polite to her than the other orderlies. She was a large woman, and I was determined not to make her angry—I had a suspicion she might hit me. I also exercised good manners around her because I didn't want her to think that I was a racist.

I took a bite or two of the bland sponge, and she appeared to approve. I decided to go ahead and ask. "Gildette, are you from Nigeria, by any chance? Or maybe Cameroon?"

For a moment, she didn't say anything. Then, to my surprise, she gave me a look of annoyance. "I grew up in Brazil."

I thought of telling her about my two trips to Africa, but decided against it. "Gildette, do you know where my sister Ruthann is?"

"Ruthie is out in the hallway with Devon. She's practicing for this morning's race." She laughed. "I tripped over her practice pylon."

"That sounds dangerous." I sampled the canned pears. Lukewarm, devoid of flavour. I used a sip of water to get them down. "Do you think she has a chance?"

"I'm not sure," Gildette said, drawing the curtains and opening the window a crack. "Only a few women are competing."

I wasn't surprised, but still a bit concerned. I could imagine some of the younger men—those in their fifties—having an unfair advantage against my vulnerable older sister. Maybe some who don't even normally use a wheelchair would enter the race. I pictured some kind of disorderly Geritol-class version of bumper cars—chaos on the gymnasium floor.

"Is there a prize?"

"Yes. The winner gets the meal of their choice every dinner for the rest of the week. Doesn't that sound nice?"

I couldn't pretend, even with Gildette. "I suppose it would be if the food here were edible," I replied, pushing my tray forward slightly.

"Hey!" Gildette raised her voice. "My sister works in the kitchen."

I looked down.

"Cassandra, do you want me to take you to the auditorium when it's time for the races?"

"No, thank you, Gildette. I will manage." Cane or no cane, I was determined to take the stairs myself. Elevators are for lazy people.

Gildette took my tray and walked out the door. I heard my sister's voice in the hallway. She sounded giddy. "I turned the corner on my own!" she said with clear joy.

"You did a great job." Devon's voice was tender and strangely emotional. "Downstairs, you'll have a bit less room if the guys on either side reach the pylons at the same time—so you may still need a bit of help."

"No one will keep up with me!" Ruthann giggled like a little girl. They sounded like a parent and child—an observation that filled me with unease.

Their voices grew louder, then started to recede. Ruthann and Devon walked past the door to our room and continued toward the elevator. I decided to wait before heading downstairs, so as not to run into them in the hall. *Who knows*, I thought, *maybe she will be victorious.* Perhaps I could talk her into sharing her special dinners with me.

It may have been the slowest race in history, but believe it or not, my sister won. Although she was the only woman to compete, most of the contestants were her own age, some even in their eighties. My fears aside, there had been no ringers. I was just happy she didn't hurt herself.

I'd sat in an isolated corner and intended to make my way over to Ruthann to offer congratulations, but before I knew it, she was spirited away—presumably off to the dining hall with the staff and her two runners-up. They were entitled to the first pieces of cake. At their age, these old people should not be eating chocolate cake. I decided I would retire to my room for a rare moment of quiet.

The gymnasium floor was rubberized and my cane sank into it, if only by a quarter-inch or so, but it was an unexpected and uncomfortable sensation. I slowed right down to avoid losing my balance. The path toward the exit got crowded. I was fighting the current: everyone was headed for the cake, and I just wanted to get out of there.

I turned away, startled by a yell and a loud moan from the middle of the dispersing crowd. Good grief—it was my raunchy neighbour Ethel Grennier. She'd shit her pants again. Several of the women next to her lurched away, while the one closest to her just patted her on the back softly while waiting for the orderlies to come over. I imagine the Good Samaritan was breathing through her mouth.

A discarded wheelchair rolled into my path in the ruckus. As I took a step, my foot caught inside the spokes of a back wheel, and I fell to the ground. Pain shot up my leg, from my twisted ankle to my knee. While I felt tears streaming down my face, and

I hurt too much to be embarrassed, I tried not to make a sound. I froze on the floor, wishing I could disappear, holding my eyes tightly shut.

A pair of strong hands lifted me up slowly and carefully, setting me into the very wheelchair that had been to blame for my fall. I opened my eyes. It was Rory. He left me for a minute, then came back with a glass of water and some painkillers, which I swallowed quickly, eager to restore my sense of control. "Let's go up to your room," Rory said quietly, heading toward the elevators.

"Thank you, Rory," I replied, humbled.

We rode the elevator in silence, then Rory wheeled me down the hall. When we entered the room, I realized immediately we were not alone. The privacy curtain—normally never used—had been pulled around Ruthann's bed. I heard her make a strange hissing sound.

Placing my hands onto the back wheels of the chair, I pulled into the room on my own, a pain wrenching my right leg. I wheeled up to Ruthann's bed and pulled on the curtain.

Ruthann lay on the bed, clothed, while Devon stood above her. He was stroking her cheek with one hand, the other out of sight in front of him. She had one hand on her breast and the other at her side.

Devon's body jerked toward me, slowly chased by his lazy blue eye. He'd been groping himself in his tight scrubs. He moved the hand away. I pushed forward in the chair till I hit his foot, then reached forward and punched him in the lumpy crotch. Devon yelped, grasped himself between his legs with both hands, and ran out of the room. Ruthann began to scream.

I turned from her to face Rory. "I want to report this to the authorities," I said, rolling back to my own side of the room. Ruthann's yelps turned to loud, sputtering cries.

Rory looked stunned. "I'll speak to the floor manager right now," he replied, and turned to leave the room, closing the door behind him.

I sat and watched in silence as Ruthann's cries quietened and eventually ceased. She turned her face toward me, red-eyed. She spoke through clenched teeth.

"I asked him to touch my face. That's all that happened."

I stared at her, filled with pity.

"Touch is sacred."

I couldn't believe my ears. "Ruthann..." I began.

"Call me Ruthie!" she yelled back. "That's what I like to be called."

Looking away, I wheeled out of the room, heading for the elevator, for the rose garden.

Is this sort of behaviour to be my fate as well, when I'm as old as Ruthann? So desperate for touch that I would allow myself to be stroked by a filthy opportunist, a pervert? I certainly hoped not. For I could not imagine anything quite as tragic and awful as that.

THE
EXCHANGE

MIKE MARTELL'S EYES NARROWED as he looked down at little Roddy Kostenko. Mike had a good six inches on Roddy. He was taller and chubbier than the small-framed boy. He leaned over Roddy and scowled. His hair was greasy, and he wore a dirty brown vest. "If you don't bring me Bettina's panties by tomorrow, you're dead meat, Stinko!"

Mike was never without his lanky cohort Eddie Wallace. The second boy's eyes were bits of coal. "Yeah, Stinko," he added, his reedy voice a lurid taunt. "No sniffing them, either."

Mike lunged forward, and with both hands, shoved Roddy, knocking him off his feet. Just as he splashed into the muddy puddle, Roddy woke to the sound of his mother's entreating voice.

Roddy turned to see her head poking in through his bedroom

door. "Get up and have a shower, Roderick. You don't want to be late for school, do you?"

Roddy shook himself from slumber, consciousness seeping in like a wet blanket tossed over him. "Yes, Mom... No, Mom." The opposite was true. No, he didn't want to have a shower, and yes, he did want to be late for school. Maybe starting at a new school was easy for someone else, some ideal boy who made friends with everyone he met. But it never got any easier for Roddy. So far, entering a new school in a new city more than half way through the school year had felt like a record low. He pulled himself to his feet and faked making his bed, only bothering to straighten the top sheet, hoping his mom wouldn't notice the misshapen lumps underneath. She would, like always—but he'd be gone by then.

He kicked the book at his feet—a Funk & Wagnalls encyclopedia (the letter P), which he'd read in bed the night before. It ricocheted off a box in the corner of the room, sending up dust and filling the air with the warm smell of stale cardboard. He still hadn't unpacked everything, though they'd been in the townhouse for a month.

"Hurry up, Rod! I need to get your little sister in and out of the tub before Grandma and Papa get here."

Roddy grabbed yesterday's pants, underwear, socks, and a clean brown T-shirt, his favourite. He trudged into the bathroom, closed the door behind him, and let the cold water run into the tub without getting in. He took his time putting his clothes on, and splashed warm water from the sink tap onto his face. Roddy soaked his short, dark hair; his mom had cut it the night before.

He ran a bar of soap over his cheeks and forehead and rubbed the white bubbles across his face, then quickly rinsed before turning off the water running into the tub. His wet hair and the smell of soap on his face would be enough to convince his mom he'd bathed. He avoided showers and baths; they made him feel like he was drowning.

Roddy meandered toward the kitchen, where his mom had a bowl of cereal waiting for him, Golden Grahams, his very favourite. Most days, he was allowed only healthy cereals—a choice between Special K or Cheerios, lest he be forced into something gross like All Bran. They got Alpen sometimes, too—but only when it was on sale. It tasted weird, anyway.

"C'mere and give me a hug, baby. Happy birthday!"

Roddy sank into his mother's waiting arms, jiggling around for a moment when one of her blonde curls tickled the side of his face. He was so wound up about Mike and Eddie's ominous warning that he'd forgotten his own birthday. Not that there had been any big plans, just Grandma and Papa driving up to Burlington. Roddy hadn't had a birthday party since he was five.

Today he turned nine. For the past couple of years, his mom— and his dad, before he was switched to the late shift at the Ford plant—had taken him and a friend to the fast-food restaurant of his choice for his birthday. But they'd only lived here for three weeks—he didn't have any friends yet. Burlington was different from St. Catharines, the town where he'd grown up. Kids were tougher.

He munched his Golden Grahams, relishing their distinctive

honey flavour. It was what his mom called "an acquired taste." His little sister Olive sat silent in her high chair, slowly lifting her spoon and then placing it back down in her empty bowl. Her autism made her act that way. His mother stood at the kitchen sink scrubbing a pot; when she was done, she'd feed Olive.

When he was finished, Roddy picked up his bowl and brought it over to his mom at the sink. She leaned down to kiss his cheek.

"Have a great day, kiddo," she said with a smile. Her voice was gentle and quiet, so as not to disturb Roddy's dad, who'd just gotten to sleep in their nearby bedroom. If his dad wasn't in there, Roddy thought, he could have snuck in and grabbed a pair of his mom's underwear to give Mike instead of those belonging to the notorious Bettina Inck—or Bettina Ick, as most of the other kids called her.

Karen the crossing guard loomed over him, grinning as usual. Roddy suspected that Karen would give him her panties if he asked. She was abnormally friendly, like a drunk circus clown, always telling Roddy jokes he didn't understand and strange stories about her and her husband. Roddy had seen Karen's husband once, on his first day of school, when Karen was just starting her shift. They looked a lot alike; both had that same peculiar smile.

"Hey there, little man!"

"Hi, Karen," he said with his usual reserve.

"Did you hear the one about *Star Trek* and toilet paper, Roddy?"

"You told me yesterday. They circle Uranus, looking for Klingons."

The Exchange

The light changed and she led him across Hampton Heath Road. The schoolyard was three short blocks away on Croydon Road. Roddy had no books to carry—he'd finished all his homework in class before the bell rang.

Roddy ignored Karen's wave and kept going up the street, his steps unhurried in the cool spring morning. A girl with blonde ringlets and a green dress had crossed the street at the same time. With each slow step he took, the gap between them widened. Roddy counted the number of steps it took to reach the schoolyard. The less time to kill in the playground before the morning bell rang, the better. The screech of nearby brakes startled Roddy and he stopped counting.

He glanced over at the car as it lurched forward again; it was a red Volkswagen driven by a man with slick black hair and a moustache. There were three little girls in the back seat. One of them picked her nose with gusto, staring out the window at Roddy. The smallest wore a bathing suit.

Elizabeth Gardens Public School was an unremarkable shoebox of faded yellow brick, just like Roddy's last school. As he turned the corner onto Croydon and it came into view, a turbulent splash of noise became more specific schoolyard sounds with each step forward. A young girl screamed in defeat as another got dangerously close in a game of tag. The thud of a basketball smacked the tarmac. A little kid bawled after falling off the roundabout. Roddy heard the whizzing hiss of skipping ropes. Passing the jumping girls, he entered the schoolyard.

Roddy heard the jangle of the morning bell and made his way

to the back door where the grade threes and fours lined up next to Mrs Krevaziuk. The redheaded recess monitor wore a long navy-blue dress. He measured his pace so he would blend into the middle of the queue. The tougher kids usually gathered at the end of the line. Taking his place, he glanced back but didn't see Mike Martell.

Once the lineup was orderly enough to satisfy the teacher, students began to file inside and ascend the staircase to the second floor. Roddy had gotten used to the pushing and shoving and knew not to take it personally. At the top of the stairs, he veered left and marched across the cardboard-coloured carpet toward Mrs Giroux's pod.

Elizabeth Gardens didn't have separate rooms for each class; it had vast, open-concept floors divided into "pods." They didn't have lockers; they had rubber tubs in which to store their books between classes. This school had some quirks compared to Roddy's old one back in St. Catharines. Instead of "O Canada" every morning, they sang "God Save the Queen." And they recited a version of the Lord's Prayer with three extra lines added to the end.

Roddy made his way to his seat near the front as Mrs Giroux thumbed the attendance list. Her blonde hair was pulled tightly up into a little round ball at the top of her head and the brown dress she was wearing had a pattern of black clubs and diamonds. It made Roddy think of a deck of cards that had fallen into a jar of peanut butter.

Roddy glanced around and saw that Mike's seat at the back

was empty. Mrs Giroux reminded the class about the swim trip that afternoon for all grade fours and fives. Roddy didn't know how to swim well, and thoughts of the Olympic-sized pool at the Centennial Aquatic Centre up the street made him anxious. Still, his trunks were in his tub, and his mom had signed the consent form. There was no way out of it.

Roddy tuned out Mrs Giroux's announcements. He realized that Bettina Inck, who was in grade five, would be attending the swim trip. He still had no idea how to ask a girl for her underwear.

The bell rang after fifteen minutes and it was time to move from homeroom to Mr Rozinski's pod for science. The pods were separated by mobile green chalkboards. Between them was a large gap, through which a river of pupils streamed from one class to the other. Roddy walked over to the storage tubs, grabbed his science books, and headed to class.

Mike Martell stood in the gap between the pods, wearing the same dirty vest as he had in Roddy's dream. He wore it most days, actually. Roddy veered far to the right and kept walking as if nothing were wrong, though his pace was unnaturally brisk. A buffer of one or two kids separated him from Mike.

Mike stood still. He didn't shake his fist. He didn't say a thing. But he stared directly at Roddy from the second he came into view until the moment he took his seat in science class. Roddy pretended not to see him, though out of the corner of his eye, it looked as if the boy's lip was swollen. But Roddy couldn't imagine anyone in school crazy enough to take Mike on in a fight.

The lesson was about the growth stages of a butterfly, complete with a slide presentation on goatweed larva. They looked like hairy, stretched-out moles that throbbed. Roddy felt a spitball hit the back of his head during the slide show. He ignored it. He knew it was Aamir, who sat three seats behind him. Aamir used to get picked on by Mike and the others because of his Pakistani accent. Attention was drawn away from him when the new kid arrived, and he wanted to keep things that way. But Aamir wasn't a very dedicated harasser. With someone like that, Roddy had learned it was best not to give them any kind of reaction. After three spitballs, including one Roddy suspected was still stuck in his hair, the onslaught ended.

The combination of the gross larva visuals and someone nearby farting a bunch of times made Roddy feel sick to his stomach. The class ended and he headed back to homeroom to drop off his book, breathing through his mouth to avoid the smell.

He stood by the tubs and felt a set of fingers press down hard and pinch his shoulder. Mike's lips were an inch away from his ear. His breath was funny. Roddy thought the odour was a cigarette, though he found that hard to believe.

"Got the fucking underwear yet?"

Roddy shook his head.

"Get them for me. I don't care if you have to rip them off her."

Roddy's shoulder twitched under the pressure. Mike squeezed harder and Roddy winced.

"Got it?"

He nodded. Mike shoved him to the floor and walked away. Other kids stepped around his body.

Time for recess. At the edge of Mrs Krevaziuk's class, Roddy turned right instead of left. He headed for the farthest set of stairs. Exiting the building from the grade-two doors meant he could avoid Mike and Eddie if they were waiting for him outside the normal door.

Bettina sat in the playground by the fence reading. Roddy took a deep breath and walked toward her mass of black curls.

Bettina wore round-rimmed glasses with large frames and a simple maroon-coloured dress that looked like it hadn't been bought in a store. Roddy wondered if her mother had sewn it herself—or maybe even her grandmother. Then he remembered the rumours. Bettina's mother had taken her own life when the girl was five years old. She lived alone with her dad in a small house, in the poor neighbourhood a dozen blocks east of his own family's rented townhouse on Lakeshore.

As he approached, he saw her book was illustrated with colour pictures of flags of the world. He'd signed the same one out of the school library in St. Catharines the year before. She was studying the book in silence. Roddy leaned over.

"That's Martinique," he said, looking at the periwinkle flag on the page in front of her. It looked like the flag of Quebec except, instead of fleurs-de-lys, it featured the white outline of a coiled snake in each of the four corners.

"It's not an official national flag," she replied without looking up. "Martinique is considered a part of France."

Roddy nodded, impressed. Bettina gestured for him to sit. He crouched beside her, bolstering himself with one hand on the chain-link fence. The book was organized by region. Bettina turned several pages without saying a word, moving from the Caribbean over to Asia. She leafed past the page for Nepal—whose unusually shaped flag was Roddy's favourite—but stopped at the sight of the flag of Bhutan. A white dragon straddled a diagonal line along the centre of the banner, demarcating a yellow triangle above it and an orange one below.

"It looks like it's swimming between a sea of pee and an ocean of diarrhea."

"Um," Roddy replied. Actually, the colours had something to do with the Buddhist religion, but he didn't remember the details. Maybe it wouldn't be hard to ask her after all. Bettina was smart—but also pretty weird.

"Are you going to the Aquatic Centre after lunch?"

Bettina flinched. "Yes. But I hate swimming. I hate that place."

Roddy swallowed. "Are you wearing underwear?"

Bettina closed the book and looked at him.

"Will you lend them to me?"

Bettina continued to stare. Her face was placid, her eyes empty pools of blue.

"If I don't give them to Mike Martell, he says he'll beat the crap out of me."

Bettina frowned at the mention of the bully's name. "Mike lives next door to me. I don't like him." The recess bell rang and she stood up.

"Will you lend them to me?" Roddy repeated, desperation creeping in.

"You can keep them." She turned toward the school doors. "After lunch," she added, walking toward the building while other kids around her ran in the same direction.

Roddy walked back to school after lunch enjoying the residual taste of fried Spam and Velveeta sandwiches.

Grandma and Papa had arrived at the townhouse. Grandma played cards with Roddy's mom while Olive spun a plastic plate on the linoleum floor. They talked about where to go for dinner that night, and Roddy picked Arby's. He liked roast-beef sandwiches, as long as they made him one without mustard.

His grandfather napped on the living room couch, a wrestling match blaring on the TV a few feet away. Mom gave Roddy a special cupcake with tiny silver candied balls sprinkled all over the vanilla icing. Then it was time to go back to school.

Karen the crossing guard tried to tell him another joke—something about a priest, a phone booth, and a cantaloupe—but Roddy just nodded politely. The bus was already waiting in front of the school. Roddy went inside to get the bag containing his swim trunks. He stopped in the boys' room on the way back outside to take a pee. The empty bathroom had three floor-length urinals and a large round fountain-style wash basin with a foot pedal, designed to allow multiple boys to stand around it and wash their hands at the same time. Roddy entered a stall and locked it behind him.

As he was finishing, he heard the washroom door open. He

hoped it wasn't strange old Mr Hyder. The rotund Hungarian janitor once came into the room and heard Roddy urinating into the toilet. He banged on the door and told the boy he needed to use a urinal "to do that." He hadn't tried to peek or anything, and had left the room once he was satisfied Roddy was peeing the right way for a boy. But still, the experience unnerved Roddy. Maybe it was outside of Mr Hyder's sense of the order of things, but Roddy liked a bit more privacy.

He heard footsteps and recognized a pair of unwelcome voices. One of them was high and sounded like a whiny girl.

"Ya think he's gonna do it?" said Eddie.

Roddy heard the sound of flies unzipping, followed by noisy streams of urine. He quietly shifted his feet so his shoes wouldn't be visible in the gap under the stall door.

"He better." Mike's reply was low and gruff. He added, "If I don't bring them home tonight, my dad's gonna give me a lot more than a fat lip."

Roddy held his breath.

"We'll scare him. Then he'll do whatever we say. If he was here right now, I'd flush his head down the toilet!" One of the boys let out an ugly hyena laugh.

"Why bother? We'll just tell him that's what we're going to do. That should be enough. Besides, he could just hold his breath while the toilet flushed. Getting your head flushed isn't really that scary."

Neither boy washed his hands. Roddy listened to the slow squeak of the door closing.

The Exchange

The swimming pool was the size of a car lot. Roddy felt small. His eyes stung from chlorine in the overheated, steamy air. He wiped sweat from his forehead and turned toward the man approaching him and the other kids.

He didn't look that old to Roddy—maybe the same age as his own dad—but the swim coach had wrinkled skin that was cross-hatched like a meat pie. Roddy wondered if that's what happened if you lived underwater.

The coach wore a bright red Polo shirt and shorts the colour of a brown-paper bag. A large silver whistle dangled around his neck on a white cord. He shook the hand of the group's hairy chaperone, burly Mr Rozinski, and then turned to face them.

"My name," he pronounced slowly in accented English, "is Sergei Hamatov. Under my tutelage, you can become a championship swimmer." The coach intoned at length about his glory days coaching championship swimmers decades ago.

Roddy stopped listening. He'd been embarrassed to undress in the change room in front of the others. A boy named Scott had wrapped his towel around his waist and then changed into his swim trunks underneath the towel. Relieved, Roddy did the same. Mike and then Eddie had taken all their clothes off, Mike loudly proclaiming, "We're all men here." Roddy had looked away.

The first fifteen minutes were spent dividing the class into two groups based on ability. Since Roddy only knew how to dog-paddle, he ended up in the Tadpole group. He didn't know any of them, but they all got along, happy to be in the shallowest part of the pool. Olga, the coach's assistant, had severe features but a gentle voice. She told the half-dozen boys and girls in Roddy's group that their simple goal was to get over their fear of the water.

"Let your worries wash away," she said in accented English. "Water is your friend."

Roddy closed his eyes and allowed himself to float in the pool. He tuned out the splashes and noisy shouts from the deep end, where advanced swimmers received diving instructions from Sergei.

Then he felt a hand cover his face and another grab his chest, pulling him underwater. Panicked, he thrashed around to free himself, but the grip on his chest was too tight. A fat belly pressed up against his back. His trunks were yanked down, and he felt a spasm of pain as someone in front of him kneed him in the crotch. His bare testicles ached, and a yell filled his mouth with water. He tried to open his eyes, but the chlorine stung too much.

As soon as it started, it was over. All the hands let go, and he splashed to the surface, coughing and gasping for air. Roddy opened his eyes, pulling his trunks back up. Olga stood at the other end of the pool talking to Sergei. A few feet away, Eddie Wallace snickered. Mike Martell hovered right in front of him, leering. Without thinking, Roddy reached forward and launched his fist at Mike's face. Mike shook from the blow but didn't make a sound. He looked surprised. The other Tadpoles stared and blinked.

Roddy adjusted his trunks and dog-paddled to the nearest

ladder out of the pool. He looked at the round clock on the wall; the swim class was almost over. With rubbery legs, he headed for the change room. As he approached the door, he noticed Bettina leave the pool as well.

In the empty change room, Roddy didn't bother hiding his nakedness under a towel as he changed back into his shorts and T-shirt. He'd never hit anyone before, except for slapping Olive once when they were younger.

As Roddy left the change room, Bettina stood outside. She too had changed quickly, replacing a flowered bathing suit with the plain maroon dress she had on earlier.

She grabbed his hand and led him to the right.

"We'd better be quick," she said, leading him to an unmarked door in between the boys and girls change rooms. She turned the brass knob and opened the door. Roddy hesitated for a second, and she gave him a gentle push, urging him inward.

"We don't have much time."

They were in a small storage closet with a cement floor, blue-tiled walls, and a light bulb over their heads. It reeked of soap, evoking the feeling of getting your mouth washed out for doing something wrong. Roddy felt a queasy sensation in his belly like he was still in the pool.

Wooden shelves held gallon bottles of pink industrial liquid soap and dozens of stacked rolls of toilet paper sealed individually in wax paper. Near the door, there was a padlock and a rusty outsized key ring. Roddy saw the door had a latch for the padlock. On one wall, a poster labelled "Playboy: Miss April" featured a nude blonde woman. The hair where her legs met was a different colour from that on her head.

Roddy looked away. He'd never seen an adult undressed before except once, when he saw his dad in the bathroom shower by accident. He'd never seen a naked girl.

There was barely enough room for the two of them in the closet; only a few inches separated them. Roddy was nervous, but Bettina spoke plainly.

"I'll need to wear your underwear if I give you mine."

They both turned away from one another. Roddy unbuttoned rapidly and took off his shorts, removed his green Hanes, and pulled his shorts back up. He stared at his grey running shoes the whole time. Her dress-clad bum brushed against his for a quick moment as she bent down to take her panties off. Roddy shook with nerves and shame. His blush deepened, and he stepped aside an inch to give her more room.

"How did you know to come here?" Roddy asked, still facing the wall.

"I've been in here before."

They turned to face one another, and Bettina held her plain white panties out to him. Roddy picked them up by the waistband. It didn't feel right to touch a girl's underwear. He wanted to get the panties out of sight. He began to stuff them into his back pocket when the door opened from outside.

There stood Sergei Hamatov. Behind him were all the kids from class, dressed, in their shoes, plastic bags or knapsacks in hand, ready to board the bus back to school.

Sergei clutched the doorknob in one barnacled hand while the other grabbed at the whistle dangling around his neck. "What are you children doing in here?" he stuttered.

"You children?" Bettina stepped forward. "You know my name is Bettina. We live on the same street. So does he," she added, pointing to Mike Martell, who looked down. The children standing nearest Mike stepped away.

Bettina turned to Roddy. "Sergei and Mike's dad are friends."

Roddy walked up to Mike. In his outstretched hand were Bettina's panties.

"You said you'd flush my head down the toilet if I didn't get you these." He thrust the cotton underwear up at Mike's face, but the bigger boy made no attempt to take them.

"You imbecile!" Hamatov shouted at Mike. His whistle pendant shook. "Why would you bother this innocent girl?" He lunged forward and smacked the boy's face, leaving a big red mark in the shape of his splayed hand.

"We will find your teacher and speak to him about this. And with your father!"

At that, Mike began to blubber out loud. The Tadpoles stared and blinked as Mike started to cry. No one else moved. Sergei grabbed the boy's neck and jerked him back to the change room. The beet-faced Russian turned to face the rest of the class. "Stay here and wait!" He kicked open the change-room door and pushed Mike inside.

Roddy turned to Bettina. "Let's go," he said. He headed down the corridor toward the Aquatic Centre's front entrance, and she followed quickly, bending down discreetly to pick up her underwear. As she caught up with Roddy, she put them in his back pocket.

The front doors had windows reinforced with a hatch of thin metal wires, embedded in the glass like translucent graph paper. Roddy pushed them open and they both stepped out. It had rained since they were in swim class, and the grass and sidewalk were both damp.

Roddy turned to Bettina.

"It's my birthday. Do you want to come over? We're going to Arby's for supper."

Bettina nodded. They passed the school bus and walked south. Bettina took Roddy's hand. He squeezed it. Together, they headed for home.

THREE
TUESDAYS
FROM NOW

Dude, will you accept $500 to penetrate me?

Ben's Craigslist ad hadn't said anything about payment. He'd only placed it because he was feeling lonely. Still, he was intrigued by this response as he scanned his emails from his phone in the locker room. Right next to him, some outsized gym-rat let out a long, low fart as he yanked his skid-marked shorts down to his ankles.

Keep it classy, bro. Ben turned to avoid the fumes, stashed his phone in his locker, and grabbed his towel. Minutes later while soaping up, Ben gave the proposition some thought. Despite being naked, this contemplation didn't cause arousal; rather, he was calculating the cost per minute. With a well-paid day job as a fundraiser at a pediatric oncology charity, Ben didn't need the cash. But $500 for ten minutes' work! Ben was sure he could last twenty if someone was paying that kind of dough. He'd just think about his grandmother. Or his gerbil.

Ben had a couple experiences with sex for pay in his early twenties. Once an older guy with a moustache and wedding ring offered him a hundred bucks for a blowjob in a bus station men's room. The other time, it was Ben who paid. A random homeless guy chatted him up on the street, looking to sell a transistor radio for ten bucks. Ben offered fellatio instead. Handing him the ten after servicing him between two parked cars in a secluded lot, Ben said, "Keep the radio." That guy had a big one. Didn't smell too bad for a homeless person, either. Kind of like soil from a flower garden.

Ben kept to himself at the gym but was unself-conscious in the locker room. He had a decent bod, and he knew it. He dried off at his locker and put himself back together quickly so he wouldn't be late for work. He checked his phone again for the time.

Fuck it, he thought. *Why not?* He idly wondered what he might do with a spare 500 bucks but couldn't come up with anything. The idea made him feel a bit greedy, actually. But he knew this would make an interesting story to tell Charla. It would give them something to discuss instead of her tedious workplace drama. For someone as smart as she was beautiful, Charla could probably have a lot more control over her life. But no, she was stuck in a dead-end job with a boss she called "the spawn of Satan." She worked at an agency that gave money and subway tokens to former prisoners. Her last boyfriend was a total charity case too. How do-gooder is that? Not to mention boring. But Ben loved having a friend to whom he could tell *everything*. Well, maybe almost everything.

Ben wrote the guy back and said he only did "outcalls"; he'd seen that word in real escort ads before. Then he scrammed from the gym and joined the masses swarming the nearest subway entrance. The would-be john must live on the Internet because a response came back before Ben had even descended the subway entrance and lost signal. He had included a low-res selfie this time. Handsome, with a shaggy goatee, blue-green eyes.

I use a wheelchair. Got a problem with that? I'm on Skype. Ravercub77. Message me.

Ben resolved to write him back from work and got ready to hop on the next southbound train.

Got your email. Looking good there.

thx
listen
u been with a guy in a chair before

No.

its the same. i can run you over if ur boring though

LOL

        i need to get fucked raw so bad, i have 400 bucks

I only play safe, cool?

        ok, if you don't do it bareback maybe 300 then

Sure.

        u sound like a goody two shoes
        youll fuck a guy in chair, u dont care about the money
        r u sure ur a real top

I know how to fuck.
I've got references if you want. :0)

        u sure you dont want it raw
        my bf has a big fat cock and he always breeds my hole
        leaves it leaking with all his hot seed

You've got a boyfriend?

        yeah wtf you surprised or something
        me a poor crip all by myself until you come along

Chip on your shoulder much?

Three Tuesdays from Now

Just didn't know why you are after me then.

> he lives in edmonton
> I told you he has a nice big tool but
> it doesn't reach all the way to toronto

LOL

> your ad said you wanted nsa right
> this is def nsa, gonna move to edmonton next month
> but I'm horny for cum now

What's your boyfriend gonna think?

> he knows the score, I met him on here lol
> ok so maybe we make it 100 for u to fuck me
> u sure u dont want to fuck me raw
> i like cum squirting inside me
> a lot

I would rather be safe but let's see what happens.
Why do you keep changing the price?

> im just negotiating. whats wrong with that
> do you think im broke or poor

You know what?
I don't need the money.

even better
let's just do it for free then

You seem like a nice guy.

oh ffs, are you getting all wimpy on me
ur a real top right … i just need it up the ass bad
i like rough sex

I can be very dominant.
I'm not just a "goody two shoes" …

but ya are blanche, ya are

What?

never mind

My name is Ben.

raimundo here

I could come over tomorrow on my lunch hour.

bring it on if youre tough enough
no rubbers is better

Dr Jong-Essex was the whitest Korean guy Charla had ever met. He dressed like a Bay Street lawyer and had perfect elocution to match. His parents, she assumed, were Canadian-born like hers.

"Your numbers are great as usual, Ms Chua," said Jong-Essex. "Nothing to worry about. We can probably keep you on this same drug regimen for at least a decade." He paused and fingered a paperweight on his desk. It was a miniature of a famous Henry Moore sculpture, made of shiny reflective metal.

Her viral load had been undetectable for two years. T-cells, over a thousand. "That's healthier than most HIV-negative people," the doctor reminded her. She saw him twice a year for blood tests and an annual flu shot. Each visit, the shelving unit next to his desk featured a new photo from his most recent international cruise. This time, she could see the Sphinx behind him and a husky white guy with a trim beard. *That must be his lover.* Charla went on meds as soon as she'd found out. She'd probably had the virus for a few years already, Jong-Essex said, so in terms of microscopic battles to be fought and won inside her bloodstream, she figured she'd come out swinging. While she generally kept her medical information to herself, Charla had told her bestie, Ben. They talked about almost everything, and he knew a few poz guys. Her dad knew; he was surprisingly tranquil about it. Charla sensed that she and her father both had the same unspoken thought: it's good your mother is dead so we don't have to tell her this. She'd come unhinged. Needlessly.

She would have told Erich, the guy she got it from, if he were around. They dated for nine months and shot up together a couple dozen times. Charla was never a junkie herself. She was…what did they call it in that Al Pacino movie? A chipper. A part-timer, a weekend warrior.

And a Tuesday here and there. She only got high with Erich; he shot her up each time. It would have seemed irrational not to share the needle; she was already letting him cum inside her. If anything, fixing together felt like a form of bonding. Their last month together, he couldn't get it up anyway, and the warm downer sensation from a nice hit replaced sex as their communion. She didn't blame Erich and doubted he even knew he was infected. Did he give the virus to her—or did she take it from him? Did it matter?

One day, he told her he was moving to Thailand. The next, his possessions were gone from her Little Italy apartment, and she never saw him again. Never got high again either. She took a few days off work and locked herself in her bedroom. Charla had never bought dope herself and saw no reason to start. She missed it for quite a while, though. Especially on Friday nights after a long week in a claustrophobic office with her bipolar boss Patti.

"Ms Chua…Charla?"

"Yes, doc." She'd tuned him out.

"Is there anything else you'd like to discuss today?" Cufflinks glinted with reflected light as Dr Jong-Essex put down the iPad he'd been reading her test results from.

"What if I want to get pregnant?" Charla cracked one of her knuckles loudly as her left hand grabbed at her right. The office had a vaguely minty smell, and she noticed this for the first time as she waited for his response.

"Five of my patients have had healthy, HIV-negative babies so far this year. I'd be thrilled to make that six. Is there someone new in your life?"

"No," she said, more primly than she intended. Feelings that she would easily spill to Ben over beers, Charla still felt weird bringing up with her doctor. She'd been referred to Jong-Essex after her initial diagnosis, after Erich disappeared, after the miscarriage. She had been thinking about motherhood ever since then. On some levels, she was glad Erich was gone, along with the instability his addiction could sometimes engender, but something still felt missing from her life. In fact, she wished she could change everything.

The doctor looked up from the notes he was typing into her file on his laptop. "You don't have a hep C co-infection, and your viral replication is minuscule because of excellent adherence to your meds. Your chances for a successful pregnancy are as high as anyone else's." He seemed to get excited. "I want you to see Dr El-Assaad upstairs," he chirped. "She's an expert on HIV and fertility."

Charla hadn't even had sex in a long time. Two years and three months, to be exact. She hadn't been sure how to approach the idea of sex since her diagnosis. She didn't feel dirty, just uncertain. Who could she trust to lay herself so bare?

"I'm not sure I'm quite at that point yet." Her hand in the pocket of her black blazer, Charla picked up a quarter that lay there and toggled it back and forth between her thumb and fingertips. The ridged metal disc felt cold in the air-conditioned room.

"How about this," Jong-Essex suggested, typing rapidly on his keyboard. "What if we set up the appointment as a general information session? Let's start to get you some useful tips now, even if you don't use them immediately. If you decide you really don't want to attend, you can cancel with forty-eight hours' notice." He stared at the screen for a moment, then reached for a card and his pen. "She's free three Tuesdays from now at seven a.m."

Charla nodded, dropping the quarter in her pocket and warding off a slight, unexpected tremor.

"When you *are* ready to get pregnant," he added, "there are ways to do it safely for you, your partner, and your baby. Maintaining your low viral load is the most important thing in terms of keeping your virus to yourself, so don't miss a pill. And until then, just continue to play safe." He then reached into his desk and handed her three condoms along with the appointment reminder.

The doctor meant well, but he sounded like a high-school guidance counsellor. Charla tried to imagine the good doctor porking his fat lover, efficiently deploying a prophylactic then drilling at his big white ass like an oilman looking for black gold. She felt a twinge of jealousy at the thought of such intimacy and stood up abruptly to leave.

Jong-Essex shook her hand, as he did at the end of every

appointment. On her way out, Charla felt a low, dull ache in her side. In the elevator, she closed her eyes and tried not to think of anything. Heroin had been good for that at least.

"The white one with the v-neck, please." Raimundo gestured toward a thin cotton T with a plunging neckline.

"Showing off the chest hair today? I see." Dave plucked the shirt off the hanger with a muscled, green-inked forearm and plunked it onto the bed next to Raimundo. "Pants?"

"My black sweats. No undies."

"You must have a hot date if you're going commando." Dave lifted the shirt over Raimundo's head and over each of his short arms. Raimundo could smell the lingering scent of fresh soap on his attendant's face and neck; it smelled like Irish Spring.

"I'm just trying to keep things simple for later, buddy. The less clothes you put on, the faster they come off, you know what I'm saying?"

"Makes sense, Ray." Dave was one of the attendants at the co-op; he usually worked mornings. Raimundo liked the guy. He was professional but still fun. Not every attendant was the same—some were unfailingly polite, but stiff as a board. Raimundo appreciated people who, like himself, had a bit of spunk to them. *Why make life boring?*

Dave pulled the short cotton pants off a shelf and then helped put Raimundo's truncated sweats on, one leg at a time. Raimundo had a bit of a chub already, which Dave appeared to pretend not to notice. Raimundo tried not to focus on the slow sensation of engorgement for the moment; he would let Dave get his work done and get out of there.

Apparently the gayest that Dave ever got was watching *Glee* with his wife once a week, but Raimundo would occasionally give him glimpses into queer culture—only when it was practical for himself, not for any kind of shock value.

"Need some condoms by the bed?"

"Nope, I told him to bring some," Raimundo lied. "One last thing, please." He gestured with one arm toward the small glass bottle of Rush on the desk by the computer, a red-inked lightning bolt strewn across its yellow plastic label. Dave unscrewed the bottle and held it under Raimundo's nostrils one at a time for a sniff, before replacing the cap and putting the bottle back in its place. The odour of the sex-enhancing inhalant wafted through the room, its distinctive scent evoking a pile of unlaundered gym socks.

"Thanks a lot, man. That's all I need for now. Maybe put on the news on your way out." Raimundo's face flushed as he smiled, his breath slowed slightly, and the throbbing between his legs renewed.

"Have a good one, Ray. Call down later if you need anything." Raimundo heard Dave walk through the living room and click on the TV, then heard the apartment door open and close behind him. Raimundo leaned forward toward the joystick and propelled his chair to the computer. He turned on the small, round webcam sitting next to the keyboard, which aimed at the empty bed. Then he backed up and went into the living room, waiting for his guest to arrive.

Magenta, green, blue, an approximation of yellow: grainy pixels shimmer and flash, trading positions. Blurred, fuzzy, they jitter, toggle off and on, resembling fireflies in motion. Amid the shifting distortion sits a man in a chair, wheels in front and rear, wearing a pair of black gym shorts. Short legs. Before him stands a man whose head is out of view, cut off at the top of the frame. He wears a business suit. He lowers his head toward the other man's; lips meet and meld. As they kiss, the suited man's fingers roam the body of the other: stubbled chin, naked chest, small arms that end in rounded tips, the back of the neck. This diffuse image moves across a flat-screen monitor next to a near-empty coffee mug and an ashtray of thin translucent glass, half-full with cigarette butts on a brown desk. In an office chair, a lone, bearded man is clad in only a grey T-shirt imprinted with the insignia of the Indianapolis Colts. One of his hands rests on the mouse pad. The other moves slowly between his thighs, like a potter kneading a fat lump of clay.

"Yeah, the muscle dude came over yesterday on his lunch hour from work."

Raimundo watched Joe use the laser pointer affixed to his glasses to spell out a question on his communication board. *Did you get what you wanted?* Joe was hilarious. So blunt.

"Hell, yeah, I did, brother—do you want to see a video of it?"

Dude no

Joe smiled and Raimundo laughed. It had started to rain on his way to Joe's, and this always messed with the mechanisms in his chair, which was annoying. Good thing he liked his best friend a lot, because he wasn't sure if the chair would start up again right away.

Tell me what happened I know you want to

"You know me too well." Raimundo loved having a friend to whom he could tell everything. "Then you can tell me about your date with Kathy."

Joe rolled his eyes, and the laser pointer scribbled the upper wall of his apartment, incidentally next to a photo of his girl-friend that was hung on the living room wall. He spelled out another response. *I don't kiss and tell like you*

"You know you love me and don't want me to change in any way." Raimundo was eager to get on with his story. "So this guy, he was all right, pretty good-looking. He took his shirt off right away like he wanted to show off his body. Conceited much, right? So we start making out and he starts playing with my nipples."

Joe interjected, *Kathy does that too*

"I thought you didn't kiss and tell," Raimundo said. "Anyway, then he starts rubbing his fingertips on the ends of my arms which drives me crazy because they're sensitive. But he wasn't like an icky flipper queen who would just be fixated on them, do you know what I mean?"

Fetish person. Joe spelled out the letters one by one, since the word "fetish" did not appear on his board.

"Yeah, exactly. One of those guys would be staring and mas-turbating onto them and everything. This was just nice, his eyes were closed while he was kissing me, and I think he just did it because he could tell I liked it. I'm a moaner. He pulled my shorts off, but I didn't let him touch me because I was so close already! He stood on the front wheels of my chair to get some oral. Lots of guys have done that, but it does require some balance, so I was impressed. Then we went into the bedroom and did it. *Au naturel* as they say!" Raimundo giggled and Joe shot him a quizzical look.

Don't you worry about catching something

"Do you and Kathy use rubbers?"

Different. She wants to have a baby

"I don't care about AIDS anymore, you know? I just don't care. I could get hit by a truck tomorrow anyway. Dennis knows I like taking loads. He was watching the whole thing on my webcam. He likes to see me getting nailed by other dudes. I'm going to be with him for good in two weeks anyway."

I will miss you when you go, friend

"Don't get all mopey on me, bro. Put yourself in my shoes. What if Kathy lived in Alberta and you never saw her? You'd want to be with her. It's called, come for a visit. I don't care if you've never been on a plane. I do it, and so can you. Are you afraid?"

With his pointer, Joe indicated his answer. *Yes*

Raimundo stared his best friend down, with an arched brow. "But are you going to come see me?"

A near-imperceptible pause, then the answer came. *Yes*

Joe changed the subject. *Think you will see this guy again*

Raimundo laughed. "He asked me on a date. Cumming right inside me made him all emotional and clingy. Ugh. I reminded him I have a boyfriend. Then I booted him out. It was fun but now it's done."

Want to watch some TV

"Okay." Raimundo drove over to the TV set and stack of DVDs next to it, relieved to find that his chair's motor wasn't on the fritz anymore. "Whatever you do, just don't say *Glee*. I fucking hate that show."

Charla expertly separated the meat from the bone of her curried chicken wing. Something to focus on, keep her mind off her nerves. She spoke loudly to be heard above the ambient noise of the bar, not to mention "Smoke on the Water" from the nearby jukebox. "Why do you think the dude kept asking if you were cool with the wheelchair?"

"I guess he's dealt with some crap before. Gay guys can be real assholes."

Charla didn't really see gays or bisexuals as especially different from straight men. She figured that they all had the capacity to be goofy or decent. Her mouth burned from the spicy wing, and she reached for the pitcher for some more Stella. "If you're so sensitive to the plight of horny men in wheelchairs, why would you take cash from this guy?"

Ben was discreetly checking out the muscular, middle-aged coach of a girl's soccer team loudly taking up an enormous table nearby. "It was his idea!" Ben's face reddened. "I figured I should accept the offer at face value. I didn't want it to seem like I pitied him for being disabled. And I didn't take the money anyway."

"How magnanimous of you." Charla threw another drumstick aside. "You're not a high-priced call boy. I'm glad you slept with this guy for free, like you'll do with almost anyone else."

"Jealous much? Anyone would look like a slut compared to you, Mother Teresa." Ben got the server's attention as she moved away from the soccer team's table, balancing a trio of empty plastic pitchers on a large tray. He made the sign to get the bill. "Truth is, I'm proud I have pretty broad tastes."

"Well, maybe you should fuck me if you're so open-minded. I've been thinking of having a baby. I can pretend I'm in a wheelchair if it would get you off."

"Are you serious?"

Charla looked away, focusing for a moment on the waitress over by the bar. She was pretty, with faint blue eye shadow; flatchested in a plain black T-shirt.

"Well, we could use a turkey baster if you're weird about it. Yes, I'm serious. I think about it a lot. You would just be a donor. You wouldn't have to have any responsibility."

Guitars duelled in an old Black Sabbath number as nearby dart players hooted at one another, slapping each other's backs. Ben finished his sudsy mug and plonked it on the tabletop loudly. "Charla, you're my best friend. I screw around with randoms on my lunch hour. Why wouldn't I have sex with someone I actually really care about?" He paused. "Yes. Baster or no baster. I'm in."

Charla looked over at her purse, then back at Ben. "I know I've been a bit of a bitch to you tonight, and I'm not sure I'm in the mood for angry sex right now. Plus you can't just snap your fingers and be fertile. There is timing and stuff to consider. I have to talk to a specialist about it. Are you seriously willing to consider this?"

"Well, were you actually going to suggest we go back to your place and have a trial run?"

"No, but maybe we can just talk about it?" Charla hadn't had any company in her apartment at all since Erich had left.

Ben paused. "Well, the dude in the wheelchair dumped me, so I guess I'm free tonight."

"'The dude in the wheelchair.' Don't you even know his name?"

"Ray. *Ray* dumped me."

"What do you mean he dumped you? I thought it was just casual sex."

"Yeah, you're right. All he wanted was a sperm donor. Just like you."

"Jesus Christ, Ben, you are such a fucking bitch."

"I love you too."

"So do I. Seriously. Now let's get the fuck out of here."

Ben stood up to leave. Charla grabbed a twenty out her wallet and put it down. Ben did the same, and they headed for the exit.

EAST
ON 132

THEY DROVE EAST ALONG HIGHWAY 132. To the right, dozens of red oaks reached skyward, seeking the last fading embers of the late afternoon sun. And to the left, the beginnings of the sea: the St. Lawrence broadened and ebbed outward, passing Trois Pistoles, passing Rimouski, reaching for the Atlantic. But with her head buried in a copy of *The Bell Jar,* all this beauty escaped Beth's notice. Gus shifted gears, then touched her leg gently. He turned to face the open window and belched. She smiled absently but didn't look up.

The Talking Heads' *Remain in Light* cassette had played twice and was starting to grate. Beth glanced toward the back seat, where eight-year-old Todd sat. *This is the longest drive he's ever been on*, she realized. At first, he'd been content to engage in his usual roadway pastime, writing down the license-plate numbers he found on any out-of-province plates he hadn't seen before. He kept track of the plate numbers on a set of index cards that he called his "documentation." The slogan on the New Hampshire plate, "Live Free or Die," particularly intrigued him. ("Dad, what does that mean?" he'd asked. "I don't know, bud," Gus had replied. "I think it's about the fact that slavery is wrong. Which it is," he added with a masculine air of finality.) But since crossing the Ontario–Quebec border many hours ago, they'd been faced with a uniform sea of rectangular reminders that *"Je me souviens."* Todd scribbled a thick mass of intersecting triangles on the back of an old envelope. Beth couldn't blame him if he was bored by now.

Next to her, Gus tapped out a fidgety rhythm on the hairy expanse of his leg, tugging on the hem of his denim shorts. *He must be tired after being behind the wheel all day.* He hadn't let Beth drive since they'd left Peterborough that morning. "Baby, I haven't given us a vacation since our honeymoon. Let me take care of everything." She'd been slightly perturbed by his unintentionally stifling proposal, but kept it to herself. After all, she wasn't that fond of long-distance driving.

From the back, Todd suddenly piped up, sounding surprisingly alert after all. It was time for a new game. "I spy with my little eye, something that is…white!"

"Aw, fer chrissakes, kiddo!" Gus bellowed. "That could be just about anything."

When Beth looked out the window, she knew right away what unusual sight Todd had spied. A giant white whale loomed in the distance.

"What the hell?" Gus muttered under his breath as they drew nearer. The sea mammal was afloat upon a bed of gravel off to the side of the road. A large hand-painted sign announced that they were approaching La Baleine at Parc Sirois. As if for their benefit, another three signs offered an explanation in English, their block letters announcing, "Art. Camping. Souvenirs." Next to the signs, the four fleurs-de-lys of the Quebec flag waved proudly.

"Honey, why don't we stop here and spend the night?" Beth proposed. They'd made good headway in their planned trek to Cape Breton that day, and her sore eyelids told her it was time to rest. And if she was tired, she knew Gus must be exhausted.

He pulled over without argument, slowing the car until they stopped directly in front of the white-plaster whale itself. It was at least fifteen feet high and about the combined length of their AMC Gremlin and the hardtop camper hooked up to its trailer hitch. Where one might normally expect to see a fin, there was instead a large red door with six small panes of glass flanked by two frayed lawn chairs. Its large, toothless mouth gaped open, and its painted lips were curled up in a crimson smile. Between the jaws sat an old woman wearing an orange kerchief, methodically folding sheets and placing them in a hamper.

The woman put down the linens and pulled herself slowly to her feet. "*Bonsoir!*" she called out, smiling.

"Hello..." Gus said tentatively.

Beth hoped the woman spoke English. If not, she could try to employ her own rusty high-school French. But as with the driving, she knew Gus would want to handle this himself. When they'd stopped for dinner at a *Poulet Frit Kentucky* a few hours earlier, no one would speak to him in English. While a teenaged girl at the counter stifled snickers, he pointed to pictures on the menu to get them a bucket of fried chicken and some macaroni salad. Beth realized that she didn't know the French words for macaroni salad either.

Gus continued. "Madame, could we get a hookup for our trailer for the night?"

She turned away and yelled into the mouth of the whale: "Axel, *viens'citte!*" She looked back at Gus. "My grandson Axel will help you." She smiled and returned to her mound of sheets.

A long-haired teen emerged through the bright red door. In contrast to his grandmother's weathered but fair complexion, he had soft, light-brown skin and calm dark eyes. Looking directly at Beth, he said, "Come inside—we'll get you set up in no time." Beth entered the office behind Axel. Gus and Todd got out of the car to stretch and share a bag of Doritos.

The office interior was spartan. The carpet resembled AstroTurf and had a light odour of Plasticine. Next to a green wooden chair in the small waiting area, a crate table held neatly stacked copies of the tabloid *La Voix du Dimanche*. An oval ashtray made of dark amber glass held half a dozen matchbooks whose covers bore a likeness of the whale. A colour calendar was thumb-tacked to the wall. The current photo for May 1980 featured a young-looking female singer on stage before a crowd of applauding onlookers. Beth didn't recognize her.

She turned to Axel, who flipped briskly through a ledger near the cash register. He wore a hockey jersey emblazoned with a large M and a cartoon image of a beaver chomping a hockey stick in half. The oversized shirt hung loosely off his slender frame.

"I assume that you are here in Matane for the balloon, Mrs...?"

Beth approached the antique-looking wooden desk Axel sat behind. "Luciuk. Beth and Gus Luciuk."

"Lou-chuck?"

She spelled the surname for him. "It's Ukrainian," she added by way of explanation. "Not too common around here, I suppose."

"I am Mi'kmaq," he replied. "That's not so common around here anymore either."

Beth paused, not sure how to respond. "You said something about a balloon?"

"This campground would normally be deserted at this time of year. Instead, it's half-full—because of the balloon."

The next day, Axel informed her, a hot-air balloon that had launched from San Francisco four days earlier was expected to land in a farmer's field just outside of Matane. If successful, it would be the first non-stop flight of its type to span North America.

"I'd like to know why the balloon is going from there to here, instead of the other way around!" he exclaimed. "If that were the case, I would be lining up to get on it. Matane is a nice place to visit—but you wouldn't want to live here."

Beth had never seen a balloon landing before. She thought it was the sort of thing both Gus and Todd would like.

Axel told Beth to help herself to a newspaper. "Everything

you need to know about the balloon landing can be found in the first few pages."

"And take care when you walk around this evening if you are alone," he added as she left the office. "It's Saturday night, and some of the other campers here can get drunk and rowdy. Expect a few catcalls."

Beth blushed. "I think I can take care of myself. But thank you, Mr ... ?"

He flashed her a charming smile. "I am Axel Delpeuch. If you need anything at all, please come see me."

While they drove the bumpy dirt path to their assigned lot, Beth reviewed the campground map and the brochure Axel had given her. The site boasted electrical hookups, a laundromat, and shower facilities as well as such leisure options as basketball, volleyball, and horseshoes. Both motorcyclists and leashed pets were "aloud." Camping Québec had awarded the campground two stars. *Was that out of three, or out of five?* she wondered.

She told Gus the details of the hot-air balloon landing, and he suggested that they stay in town an additional day. He looked to his son in the back seat.

"Wouldn't you like to see a hot-air balloon, kiddo?"

"Of course I would," Todd replied.

The small campsite was dotted with hard-tops trailers, soft-top campers, and various tents, but was hardly filled to capacity. They followed a series of small, spray-painted wooden signs until they reached their assigned place. The lot next to it was occupied by a large stand-alone tent, a pair of rusting motorcycles, and two men sitting at a picnic table littered with cans of Labatt 50. One of them was a large guy like Gus, but dark and swarthy, where Beth's husband was ruddy and red-haired. The man had a shaved head, and his face would have been considered handsome, were he not missing a tooth. His companion was lean but had the same dark features; his straight hair was long and greasy.

As the Luciuks got out of their car, the men were in the middle of an animated discussion. The bald one was loud and self-assured. "I don't give a shit if Darcel's black, she's a damn attractive woman—she's got the finest legs of any dancer on that show!" The other guy snorted loudly and handed his buddy another beer before noticing the newcomers. "Hey, neighbours!" he called out in a voice thickened by lager. Beth's eyes narrowed as she surveyed their disheveled campsite. Gus nodded to the men. "How you guys doing."

Todd looked quizzically at the bigger biker's shorn scalp and then walked over to where his father was disconnecting the trailer hitch from the back of the car. Beth helped Gus set up the hardtop—with Todd handing them a few of the metal poles—and then she took her son to find the communal washrooms. She glanced back at their new neighbours. The large man still sat at the picnic table, wedging a toothpick between two side molars. The tall, thin one was urinating against a nearby tree.

Todd was quiet as they moved along the path toward the facilities. After a minute, he asked: "Are those guys some kind of pirates?"

Beth ran her fingers through his hair. "Well, they do talk like sailors," she offered.

They approached a rectangular block of concrete split in two sections, with the entrances to the men's and women's restrooms right next to one another in the centre. Beth patted Todd on the shoulder. "Wash your hands and face when you're done in there, and we'll get to bed soon." The men's room door closed behind Todd, then Beth turned to use the women's. She wondered how well they'd sleep this first night in the camper.

By the time Beth and Todd got back to the campsite, the neighbours had started a bonfire. Their conversation had advanced to beer preferences. The lean one scratched at his moustache and then spat into the flames. "Back when I was working in St. John's, you couldn't go wrong with a case of Blue Star. Now, that was a beer that went down smooth. 'The Shining Star of the Granite Planet,' we used to call it." Beth smiled in their direction as a courtesy. The bald man flashed her a lurid grin in response, and she quickly turned away. The other guy horked into the pile of burning branches a second time. Beth pulled back the zippered canvas door and let Todd in ahead of her.

Gus had already hooked up the electricity and had just transferred the last of the pop cans and luncheon meat from the trunk of the car into the camper's small refrigerator. A faintly musty scent permeated the interior. They'd bought it used, and it had seen better days. Putting Todd to bed on the far side of their sleeping quarters, Beth noticed a small hole in the canvas right near his pillow. She found a Band-Aid and used it to cover the hole so sunlight wouldn't stream onto his face at the break of dawn.

She turned to see that Gus had already stripped down and was climbing under the sheets. She walked toward him, turned off the light, undressed, and joined him.

"A couple of rowdies, but harmless," Gus told her in a low voice. "The fat one is Ray, and the tall one's Rick. Two brothers from New Brunswick, partying their way to some motorcycle event in Ontario. I just hope they don't keep us up all night blabbing about titties and booze. I need some sleep." He kissed the back of her neck softly. Within minutes, he was snoring. Before long, she followed him into slumber.

In the morning, they walked over to Marie's, a small snack bar next door to the campground. Beth assumed their neighbours had stayed up late into the evening. It was well past ten, and there were no signs of life next door.

The tiny restaurant had been designed to look like a boat. The walls were decorated with marine trappings, including a miniature model of a lighthouse and a petrified starfish, both of which fascinated Todd. A French-language newspaper left lying on their table had a headline mentioning the upcoming *Référendum du Québec*. Gus was relieved to find that their waitress—a cheerful woman in her fifties whose nametag read "Yvette"—spoke English with an accent but without reservation. "We have a lot of *touristes* here," she explained as she brought them oval plates heavily laden with sausages and pancakes. "Besides," Yvette added with a toss of her curly, blonde-dyed mane, "I can communicate with anybody using the international language." Gus smirked, appreciating her sassy manner. The family ate heartily.

Later, on the way back to the campground, Beth told Gus and Todd that the breakfast hadn't agreed with her.

"My belly is cramping," she announced with a grimace. "Maybe you two should go on without me. The field where the balloon is landing is just down the road. It's supposed to be a big party there."

She touched her stomach gingerly. "I think I need to lie down for a little while. Then I can come and join you boys."

"Are you sure, babe?" Gus touched her shoulder. "Why don't we wait till you feel better, and we'll all go together?"

"I don't really think that will help much. And I don't want you to miss out on the fun." Beth didn't want to be babied—and the camper was too small to be very comfortable for the three of them, except when they were asleep.

Beth promised to join them before too long, and Gus reluctantly agreed to go on ahead. He and Todd headed up the path to have a shower. When they returned to drop off their towels, Beth was lying down. They both kissed her and then left, leaving the camper door open.

She pulled a blanket around herself tightly. It smelled of Gus's sweat; the familiar scent gave her a sense of comfort. She lay quietly in the camper and listened to Gus and Todd's voices slowly fade as they walked away. Her stomach wasn't in pain. Although this was only the second day of their vacation, she felt closed in.

Over the years, she and Gus had developed a kind of quiet intimacy. In bed, he was caring and sensitive. Whether he stroked her breasts lightly or grazed her neck or thighs with his tongue and teeth, he knew how to please her physically. The penetrative act itself usually didn't take that long. Beth got the feeling that this was because he didn't want to hurt her, either with his thrusts or with the weight of his hefty body on top of her more petite frame. She didn't know how to tell him that he didn't have to be so gentle. The nature of their habits and routines had been unspoken for so long.

Beth drifted off to sleep. She dreamt that she and Gus were in their bed at home and that someone was watching them through their bedroom window. She woke up with a start. The sun's rays shone through the camper's open door, but no one was staring inside.

Slowly, she roused herself and glanced at her watch. It was noon, and the balloon was expected to reach Matane soon. By now, everyone in town must be in that farmer's field waiting for it to touch down. Sticking her head outside, she saw that the campground was deserted. The broad solitude pleased her. Beth threw on a pair of shorts and a T-shirt and grabbed a beach towel lying beside the bed. She stepped outside and walked up the path toward the showers.

After a minute, she heard some rustling noises behind her, followed by a low whistle. Ray, the large bald biker, was coming up the path with a white towel draped across his shoulder. "Howdy, ma'am," he said, his voice a low rumble. She nodded in response and kept walking, feeling his gaze tracing the outline of her bare legs. By the time she reached the entrance to the facilities, he'd caught up with her. He didn't say another word, but surveyed her body in silence for another moment. Then he adjusted his crotch casually, as if he'd just scratched an itch. With that subtle, brazen gesture, he pushed the men's room door open and walked in without looking back. Beth stood outside for several seconds. Then she followed Ray into the men's room. Behind her, the door shut slowly.

Adjusting her shirt, Beth walked out of the men's room and stepped out into the sun—and bumped right into Axel, who stood in front of her with a mop in one hand and a bucket holding a can of Ajax in the other.

They both froze, staring at one another. Then Beth turned toward the ladies' room and Axel stepped into the men's. He propped the door open with the bucket. From inside, the sounds of water pelting onto tile—and of Ray whistling in the shower— could be heard.

Alone in her own shower stall, Beth closed her eyes as she lathered her face, arms, and legs. She hadn't had sex with another man since marrying Gus—until now. She'd be happy if she never saw that biker again. Still, as she rinsed her body off, a lingering ache reminded her that she'd enjoyed their rough, gritty act.

Beth left the shower stall and walked into the empty dressing room. She'd left her clothes next to an enormous mirror that stretched from the floor to the ceiling. While dressing, she studied her reflection. *I like my hips*, she told herself, touching them with her fingertips. She made some funny faces in the mirror and then laughed. Beth wondered what it would be like to have a moment alone in front of this same mirror again ten years from now. The men's room hadn't had a full-length mirror.

Walking back to drop off her towel, she saw no sign of either Ray or his brother. The whole park looked barren and abandoned. She headed out, passing the smiling whale and walking alongside the highway toward the farm. The warm sun and cool Maritime breeze caressed her skin. A red TransAm drove by, and one of its passengers shouted something at her in French that she couldn't make out. Looking up at the sky, she could already see the large blue balloon in the distance up ahead.

Before long, she came upon a crowd behind a red farmhouse, hundreds of people gathered in a field that smelled strongly of damp hay with a faint but stubborn hint of manure. It didn't take Beth long to spot her husband and son. At six-foot-four, Gus stood out in most crowds. Todd sat on his shoulders to get a better view above the throng of people. Approaching them quietly from behind, she rubbed Todd's back playfully, and then slipped her arms around Gus's belly.

"I guess I got here right on time."

"Mom! Look at the balloon," Todd cried out.

She looked up. The balloon hovered a few hundred feet from the ground. Enormous and proud, the navy-blue vessel hung in the sky as if it belonged there—as if it were not manmade at all, its rounded surfaces shining like azure satin. The balloon descended gracefully, looking for all the world like an inverted teardrop serenely sliding down from the visage of clouds.

Its two passengers—a father and son, Gus told Todd excitedly—stood waving to the crowd from a lightweight wicker crate attached to the base of the balloon by taut nylon cords. It looked like a giant picnic basket. Off to the side of the landing area, a small marching band stood in place and began to play with celebratory flourish. The crowd broke into applause as the balloon touched ground and a handful of people rushed toward it as soon as it landed.

Gus, Beth, and Todd stayed in the farmer's field for hours, mingling with the crowd of curious locals, American visitors, and assorted balloon aficionados who'd made the trek to Matane. Gus got the autographs of the two flyers for his son. On the same piece of paper, Todd documented the identification number that had been painted on one side of the balloon.

They ate corn on the cob and cups of warm applesauce sold by the farmer and his family. Beth and Gus sat on a bleacher made from bales of hay, watching Todd played Frisbee with a few local boys who spoke only French. At one point, she saw Axel and his grandmother on the other side of the crowd. The old woman smiled and waved. Beth waved back. Her eyes met Axel's.

The celebrations eventually started to subside. The family took a walk along the river and then headed back to the campground as the sun began to descend.

When they got back to the campsite, the bonfire was roaring again next door. Wearing the same clothes as they had the day before, the brothers were drunk and noisy. They quieted down for a short while when the Luciuks arrived, but by the time the family had decided to bed down for the night, they'd gotten boisterous again.

"What can I say? She loved it...she couldn't get enough. She liked it so much, she stole my friggin' underwear!" Crude bellows of laughter roared through the camper's thin canvas walls. "I guess she wanted a souvenir. I bet she's sniffing them right now."

Gus flinched. "I'll be back in a minute," he said, standing up nude in the darkened camper and pulling on his shorts. A glimmer of orange flame sparked into view for a moment when he stepped out into the night.

Completely still, Beth listened. She hoped that Todd was already asleep. She heard Gus outside, speaking to Ray and Rick in low, hushed tones. A minute later, he came back to the camper, pulled his shorts off, and returned to bed. The two men next door were silent. "I told those jokers we have a young kid over here. And he doesn't need to hear that kind of crap." Gus sighed irritably and rolled over, turning his back to Beth.

Early the next morning, they dismantled the camper and hitched it back up to the car. Not a sound could be heard from the tent next door. They drove back up to the office. Beth got out of the car and entered the white whale once more through its red door. Axel sat behind the desk.

He wrote up their bill for the two-night stay by hand. "How

did you like Matane?" His eyes met hers. "Was your visit what you hoped it would be?"

She bent down to sign the credit-card imprint on the wooden desk, then stood up and looked at Axel. "It wasn't what I expected."

"I know," he said. He reached into his pocket, pulled out Ray's large white cotton Fruit of the Looms. He let go of the briefs, and they flopped onto the desk between the two of them. They were damp, and the front was discoloured with yellow droplets. Beth stared at them for a few seconds, then looked at Axel. He was blushing. After a moment's silence, Axel laughed nervously.

"Not much I can do with these," Beth said. "Gus wears boxers."

She walked to the door of the office and turned to face Axel again. "We'll be coming back this way in a week or so. Maybe we'll spend a night here on the way home."

"I hope you do," he said. "But I may not be here by then. I've decided to move to Montreal. I'm going to stay with my cousin Francine. She's an artist." He grinned.

She smiled back at him. "Good luck, Mr Delpeuch."

"Good luck, Mrs Luciuk."

Beth left the office, got into the car, and tossed the receipt from the campground onto the dashboard. She gave Gus a kiss, and he stroked her cheek gently in response. Todd reached forward to hand her a cheese sandwich as they drove away from the white whale, slowly picking up speed.

They drove east along Highway 132. Within minutes they

reached the empty field at Dubroc's farm. Beth rolled down her window and looked to the spot where the balloon had landed the day before. She closed her eyes for a moment. Then she picked up the map that sat next to her novel on the dashboard; it was warm to the touch from the heat of the morning sun. Beth unfolded it and noted their upcoming turnoff, south onto 195. The next stop would be New Brunswick. She traced its outline on the map with the tip of her finger.

ACKNOWLEDGMENTS

This book would not have been started without the support and encouragement of Marnie Woodrow and would not have been completed if not for similarly wise and insightful contributions from Kathryn Kuitenbrouwer. Thank you to Claude Mercure and Paul Leonard for their much-appreciated editorial suggestions. Thanks to many editors who have worked with me on these stories, including Steve Berman, Maurice Mierau, Michelle Miller, Troy Palmer, and Emily Schultz. I would also like to gratefully acknowledge the financial assistance of the Toronto Arts Council and the Ontario Arts Council.

My heartfelt thanks to everyone at Arsenal Pulp for their efforts to make the book better and get it out into the world: Brian Lam, Susan Safyan, Cynara Geissler, Gerilee McBride, and Robert Ballantyne.

Thank you to my family for all their support: my mother Margaret and brother Chris and husband Jeff. Thank you to my close friends for their encouragement: Paul Schofield, Don Pyle, Jason Winkler, Wes Doherty, Paul Dubaz, and Harry Hodges.

This book is dedicated to the memory of my father Frank Syms and the memories of several individuals who were very influential during the period in which this book was written: Barrie Joseph Cossette, Patrick Duggan, Kathleen Gilbert, Melinda Morningstar, David Parnell, and Bertha Prosyk.

SHAWN SYMS is a widely published author, journalist, and critic whose work has appeared in more than fifty publications over the past twenty-five years, including *The Journey Prize Stories 21, Canadian Literature,* the *National Post,* and *The Globe and Mail,* as well as the acclaimed anthologies *First Person Queer* and *Love, Christopher Street: Reflections of New York.* He is the editor of the anthology *Friend. Follow. Text. #storiesFromLivingOnline.* Shawn was raised in Niagara Falls, Ontario, and lives in Toronto. *shawnsyms.com*